UP THE SHENANDOAH

BILL ESHENBAUGH

ILLUMIFY
MEDIA.COM

Contents

1

Loading Up

Will pulled his blanket tight around his shoulders. The cold November wind rattled his bedroom's single-pane window. Looking outside with the sky illuminated by full moonlight, he could see heavy frost covering the ground, and he knew winter would arrive soon.

In the moonlight glow, he could also see his clock showing almost four a.m. *Time to get up*, he thought as he rolled out of bed and pulled on his heavy wool socks and pants and found his shirt. Heading downstairs, he stopped at the top of the stairs to tap lightly on his mother's bedroom door. He heard her answer and told her he'd light the kitchen stove and head to the barn to prepare for the day.

In the dark kitchen, Will found the lamp on the table and the match beside it. When the lamp sputtered to life, Will went to the firewood box and pulled out kindling wood to light a fire in the iron stove. Beside the box, he pulled a page from an older newspaper, making sure it wasn't one that carried news from the war front. His father, Andrew, had been gone for over a year, ever since he joined the 14th Pennsylvania Cavalry Regiment and had fought at Gettysburg last summer.

Lighting the paper and firewood, Will soon had a nice fire heating the cookstove. He pulled on the pitcher pump a few times and was able to fill the coffeepot. Since the start of the war, coffee beans had been hard to come by, but the local grocer provided a limited supply when Will delivered fresh eggs and potatoes. Within minutes, the coffee had boiled, and Will poured a metal cupful, pulled on his boots, coat, and slouch hat, then headed to the barn.

Will shivered as he crossed the barnyard, glad that these cold November nights turned into warm afternoons, especially with clear skies and a shining sun. Will faced a long day ahead. He and Mother would take the team of horses and a wagon loaded with sixty-seven sacks of potatoes to delivery in Butler, ten miles away.

The roads would be passable since there hadn't been any rain for a couple of weeks. The owners of the general stores and taverns would be happy to see the freshly dug potatoes, which were in high demand due to the war and all the travelers and troops passing through. Will also had heard that the army sutlers were at the train station buying up provisions, horses, mules, and anything else that could be sold to the army. He figured he could sell at least twenty sacks of potatoes to the two general stores on Main Street and the three tavern owners who knew his father. Potatoes had been selling for as much as a dollar a bushel. At sixty pounds per bushel, Will had sixty-seven bushels on the wagon, so he might sell for as much as sixty dollars or more.

The barn was warm from the body heat of the three cows and four horses. Tom and Queen, the two older draft horses, whinnied softly when Will opened the door and entered the barn with his lantern lighting up the stable. Will dumped two quarts of oats in buckets for Tom and Queen and one quart for each of the younger horses, Jeff and Phil. Today, Tom and Queen would pull the loaded wagon ten miles south to Butler, on a road with several steep hills. They would be tired tonight when they made the trip back to the farm just south of the village of West Sunbury.

Will moved Bella, the oldest cow, into a stall, tied her, and fed her a scoop of corn and a fork of hay. Quickly, he fed the younger cattle corn and hay as well. Bella stood still, content to be milked while munching her morning rations, while Will filled the milk pail with swift jerks of her teats.

When Bella was milked out, Will took the brimming bucket to the small spring house and poured the fresh warm milk into a cooling jug and set it into the chilly water that ran constantly from the spring. Later in the morning, one of the younger brothers would fetch the cold jug and bring it to the house so all the family members could enjoy the fresh whole milk with their breakfast.

While the animals finished eating, Will loaded a bag with eight more quarts of oats and put it in the front of the loaded potato wagon, so he'd have two quarts each for Tom and Queen at noon and again on their way back home tonight. He also put two nose bags on the wagon so he'd have a way to feed them. Next, he gathered up wagon robes from the wall in the stable and put them on the seat so he could make sure Mother was covered against the November chill this morning. If they were late getting home that night, she'd be warmed by the blankets after the sun waned in the west.

Now close to five a.m., Will was determined to leave at six even though daylight wouldn't begin till an hour after that. The full moon would make it easy to see, and he wanted to get into Butler as early as possible. It would take at least five hours to get there with the heavy wagonload of potatoes and probably two hours to sell his load, an hour to pick up supplies, and four hours back home, making their arrival around nightfall if all went well.

When he stepped back into the kitchen, Will felt the warmth of the kitchen stove and smelled bacon frying and pancakes in the skillet. He was surprised that all the younger ones were up and dressed for the day. Mother had awakened them so they could be ready for their departure and get their instructions for the day. Albert was the oldest of them at age fifteen, a strong young man proud of his role of being left in charge. Mother was going over his work duties of the day, including tending to the hogs and chickens, bringing in the fresh milk, gathering the eggs, and then feeding the horses and cows late in the afternoon before she and Will returned. The rest of the children—Annis, James, Samuel, Alberta, Isabella, and the baby Priscilla—would be home all day without Mother for the first time. Will knew she would worry about them, but the trials of war bring on many changes, and this was just another challenge.

2

Trip to Town

Mother packed a lunch of ham sandwiches, boiled eggs, and cookies she'd made for the family. While she briskly cleared the table, washed the dishes, and gave the children instructions for the day, Will again donned his jacket, hat, and boots before heading out to the barn. He turned out the younger horses and the cattle for the day and unhitched Tom and Queen from a post in the barn. Will had grown up with horses and at twelve years old had learned to drive a team. With his father, Andrew, off at war, he'd become a skilled teamster as he worked the farm, hauled crops, and plowed fields. Now a teenager, Will stood over six feet tall and had a full head of jet-black hair and a full mustache. He was well muscled from all the hard labor of farming.

Will drove the team to the front of the house and hitched the animals to a post. He stepped down from the wagon to go help Mother gather their traveling supplies. But before he did, he covered up the big Colt .44 pistol and the Henry repeating rifle behind the wagon seat. Both guns were state-of-the-art, early advances in repeating firearms. Papa had brought these home on his last leave and taught Will how to load and shoot both.

Mother kissed each of the little children good-bye and turned to Albert with her last-minute instructions for the day. Steel-willed, Mother had been born on a ship crossing the Atlantic from Ireland and traveled as an infant by wagon through the Cumberland Gap to Western Pennsylvania. Life as a child was spent in a small cabin as her father farmed and hunted to feed his family. Born Mary Ann Dixon, the oldest of twelve children, she endured a hardscrabble life growing up on the frontier of Western Pennsylvania. Her father, James Dixon, had been trained in bookkeeping in a shop in Dublin and eventually got a job keeping the books for a general store in Butler.

⚬⚬⚬

Now, as Will and Mother loaded the last of their belongings into the wagon, the team snorted and hoofed the dirt, obviously full of energy and eager to get moving. Will gave them a bit of rein and called their names as they eased down the driveway and onto the dirt road, headed downhill and south toward Butler.

Still in darkness, the travelers began the first mile across a flat stretch and then a hillside descent, so the horses had a chance to warm up before the hard pulling that would come. They crossed a creek aptly named Muddy Creek, with Will surprised to see the unusually high water and fast current. Just beyond the small bridge over the creek, they crossed a new set of railroad tracks that led to coal mines farther north. Several hundred rail ties were stacked just east of the crossing along the road, and Will could only guess that maybe a new spur would be added to give access to a new coal mine on the hill above them.

He stopped the team to rest for a few minutes, then slapped the reins and headed them up their first hill on the trip. The sun peeked over the trees to the east, and the day promised to be fair and warm as November days often did. Tom and Queen took to their work and easily ascended their first hill of the day.

As they bumped along on the dirt road, Will said, "Mother, I hope Father will be pleased with the potato crop this year. It's the biggest we've ever had. Of course, good weather all season helped, but still, I'm so proud. Will you be writing to him soon?"

"Yes," she said, "I plan to write when we get back and let him know how well you've done. I'll assure him that he need not worry about money for us. Our sales today will be far more than he's able to send home on his army pay of twelve dollars per month, before expenses. I know he will be relieved and proud of you."

They rode along in silence for the next two miles, and it then came time to descend a steep, winding road down to a creek and another railroad track. Before starting down the road, Will again rested the team and checked his hand brake and foot brake as well, knowing he'd need them both to help the horses with the heavy load. After a few minutes, Will made the familiar clucking sound to urge them forward and start the descent.

Mother grasped the rail along the seat and braced her boots against the foot rail as she glanced down the hill. She couldn't see the bottom as the road had a sharp left-hand turn halfway down. Tom and Queen braced hard against the downward gravitational pull. The wagon groaned and the brakes squealed as Will pressed down on the rear brake controls.

Slowly they made their way, first to the sharp turn and finally to the turn to the bottom flat area. Will pulled the team to a watering trough that was fed from the stream, grateful that his team could drink cool water before starting their ascent of another hill.

⁂

By now, with the sun well up, Will guessed it might be close to ten a.m., and they were more than halfway to Butler. The next mile was a slow downhill run to the bottom of the biggest hill on the route. Will let the team set their pace, moving along with ample energy. The big hill ahead, called Stone House Hill, had been a stagecoach stop at one time but today served as home to a farmer who raised sheep that grazed the pastures on the steep slopes around the house.

After a rest at the bottom, Will set Tom and Queen in motion to tackle their toughest climb of the day. The team was up to the task, and in a few minutes they were at the top of the hill and headed for two miles of flat, winding road into Butler.

3

Day of Selling

Will, his mother, and their team arrived at their destination, a bit weary and dusty but grateful for no significant mishaps. The town of Butler was the new seat for Butler County that had been spun off from Allegheny County to the south around 1850. The war had brought robust new business to Butler, as rail lines connected Butler to Pittsburgh and the three rivers of commerce that shaped Pittsburgh. With Butler situated near substantial coal mines, iron ore, and timber, a railroad wheel manufacturing company and an iron and steel mill had sprung up. Numerous immigrants from Ireland and Eastern Europe made their way to Butler seeking jobs, along with many traders and suppliers.

As Will and Mother entered the heart of the town, the streets bustled with horses, wagons, and carriages. The sidewalks were full of pedestrians, laborers, and shopkeepers, even though it was only late morning.

Mother leaned toward Will and said in a low voice, "A rough-looking lot, these men."

Will had noticed that most were carrying rifles, and many had pistols and knives hung from their belts. He had also noticed how his mother glanced around nervously, alert to danger.

Will's first stop was at Kelly's Tavern, along the north end of Main Street. Mr. Kelly knew Will's father from before the war when he bought potatoes from him. Will had been alongside his papa as a lad on those delivery expeditions. Kelly came out immediately to greet Mother and ask of any news from Andrew at the front in Virginia.

"As much as we can tell, all is well," she answered, adding, "though news does not come as frequently as we would like. And I don't know how Andrew, at age forty, keeps up with troopers as young as sixteen."

After a bit more chitchat with Kelly, Mother told Will she was headed up the street to shop while he did business.

Kelly turned to Will and asked, "So what have you got today?"

Will pulled back a horse blanket to show off his wagonload of new potatoes.

Kelly whistled and said, "They look just fine. What do you want for them?"

"Well, Mr. Kelly," Will responded, "I've heard the market to be as much as $1.25 a bushel."

Kelly pushed his hat back and rubbed his apron. "Sorry, Will, I can't pay more than one dollar a bushel."

Will's heart pounded, feeling very much like a kid bargaining with a veteran tavern owner.

After several seconds of thoughtful silence, Will countered by saying, "I suppose I could come down to $1.10 per bushel—for an old friend of the family."

Kelly didn't say anything for quite a while and finally agreed to purchase ten bushels.

Relieved, Will shook hands with Kelly and started unloading the negotiated supply. With the haul of potatoes inside the tavern's back storeroom, Kelly handed him eleven one-dollar bills, which Will quickly folded and buried deep in a pocket of his coat.

"Will, give your father my best, and we pray he gets home safe and sound," said Mr. Kelly as they shook hands once again.

Will unhitched Tom and Queen and moved out into the street. As he proceeded up Main Street, he observed two men who seemed particularly suspicious. One was dressed in buckskin hide, and the other wore a bearskin coat, clad in all black clothing, including a large black slouch hat. He had scraggly dark hair and a huge unkempt black beard. Will decided he'd just think of them as "Buckskin" and "Blackie."

Two blocks up the street, the McCarrier General Store stood on the corner. Will turned right at the corner and then halfway down the block pulled Tom and Queen to a stop. He tied up the horses to a post and entered the front door of the general store. It was full of people shopping for dry goods, food, and even clothing. Will spotted Mr. McCarrier behind the meat counter, busy cutting an order of pork for a woman shopper. Will waited until they were finished and then Mr. McCarrier looked up and asked him if he could help the young man.

"I'm Will Eshenbaugh, son of Andrew Eshenbaugh, and I've been here with my father before the war to sell potatoes. Now I'm here today with a load to sell in town and hope you might be interested."

"Well, hello Will. My how you have grown," the shopkeeper said enthusiastically. "Is Andrew still at war and is he fine? He's always been one of my favorite people. Plus, he always raised good potatoes."

"Thank you," responded Will. "Yes, sir, Father is fine and reenlisted last year for three years. He's been in Virginia in an area he calls the Shenandoah Valley riding patrol since the Union Army marched south after the big battle at Gettysburg last summer."

"Good to hear, especially with so many troubling reports coming trickling back from the war front," he said. "Now, let's see what you have for sale today."

Will replied that he'd come to town with sixty-seven bushels and had sold ten to Kelly's Tavern. When asked how much he wanted, Will said he'd heard prices were as high as $1.25 per bushel, but for longtime customers, he'd take a little less.

"Will, you'd have to take less as I'm going to need to mark them up so I can make a profit," McCarrier said. "I'm not here for my health, that's for sure. I could take ten bushels at one dollar a bushel. That's the most I can pay."

Will thought for a moment and answered, "Mr. McCarrier, my father would want me to be fair with you, of course. The winter is likely to have many shortages as the army is buying up a lot of food. And since Mr. Lincoln will likely be reelected for four more years, some think the fighting will be the heaviest yet in the coming spring."

Will saw the shopkeeper thinking this through, and so he continued, "What with all the farmers off to war or already killed or wounded, there won't be nearly as much supply of potatoes for the year ahead. I could take one dollar a bushel if you agree to take thirty bushels instead of just ten. That way, by next spring you could be the only one around with potatoes for sale."

After what seemed like minutes of silence, Mr. McCarrier said, "Son, for such a young man, you are a natural-born sales-man. As you may recall, I have a large, cool basement under the store, and the potatoes will keep just fine down there. Get to unloading your thirty bushels, and I'll get the money. Plus, I'll send a couple of boys to help haul the bags down."

Will felt thrilled as he left the store. Here it was just early afternoon, and he'd already sold forty of his sixty-seven bags of potatoes. He untied the team and climbed aboard the wagon. They were ready, and he swung ahead and to the right and headed to the top of Main Street. There stood the majestic four-story stone Butler County Courthouse. Across the street was a park that covered a full city block. Will swung the team around the park and pulled up next to a large tavern that had the largest restaurant in the city. It was busy all day long feeding the workers and visitors from the courthouse. Will was glad he had arrived before the place would be jammed with a crowd for their noontime meal and maybe a beer or two.

Will had been here as a youngster but had heard the owner had sold the place and gone off to the war. He entered and looked around the dimly lit bar and dining area. He was taken aback to see Buckskin and Blackie sitting at a table back against the wall. They had several empty beer mugs in front of them as well as the ones they were drinking from.

Will approached the barkeep and asked if the owner was in.

"I'm the owner," the man replied. "And what might you want, lad?"

Will told him he was selling fresh potatoes and had already sold forty bushels but had more for sale.

When asked how much they were, Will gave his stock answer that he'd heard some were paying $1.25 per bushel.

The owner snorted and said, "Not in this bar. I'll take five bushels at $1.05 and not a penny more."

Will quickly agreed, unloaded five bushels, and carried them to a side door. He returned to the bar, and the owner handed him his $5.25. Will felt uneasy knowing that Blackie and Buckskin could see him, so he slid the money into his pants pocket rather than his jacket, thanked the barkeep, and headed for his wagon.

As Will pulled away, he caught sight of Blackie, who had come to the front door of the tavern and watched Will leave the building.

Mother had walked up Main Street to shop at a millinery. She picked up thread and needles along with a bolt of cloth so she could make new dresses for Annis, Alberta, Isabella, and little Priscilla.

Will and Mother had agreed to meet at the corner of Main Street and Jefferson Avenue, and sure enough, there she stood, waving and smiling. It pleased Will to see his mother's happy expression, as she didn't smile much these days, what with her husband off to the war and the burden of managing a bustling family and a farm on her own. Will helped her board the wagon, and she immediately asked how he'd done so far. Will went through the sales he'd made and the prices paid.

"I am so proud of you," she said. "And your father would be too."

She asked Will to stop at the post office so she could mail a letter to Andrew and then asked if Will could give her five dollars to include in the envelope.

He pulled in front of the post office, tied up the horses, and helped Mother off the wagon. While he waited, he saw that the Butler Federal Bank sat just across the street, and he remembered that his pal Fred Boozel had moved to Butler to work for the bank, cleaning the marble and running errands. Will decided to step into the bank and see Fred.

When he entered the bank, it felt like all eyes were on him, looking him over. Will realized how poorly dressed he was with rough farm clothes, now covered with soil from the potato bags, and he quickly removed his hat. The armed guard asked him his bank business.

"Yes, sir," Will explained. "I am in town conducting business for the day, and I came to the bank to say hello to my friend Fred Boozel, if he's here."

"Fred was sent on an errand," the guard said. "No telling when he'll be back. If you have no other business here, you'll need to move on."

Will quickly left the bank and headed back to his wagon to await Mother. He was again taken aback to see those two unsavory characters, Blackie and Buckskin, standing on the corner of Main Street and Jefferson Street. They both stared at Will. As Will stared back at them, he took note that the one he called Buckskin stood over six feet tall and had an odd crook to his left arm. He carried it high and tucked into his chest. Will wondered if the arm had been broken and healed poorly.

They made Will so uneasy that when he climbed up in the wagon, he pulled the pistol from under the burlap bag and tucked it in his waistband, where it was hidden from view but readily available if he needed it. Will thought about the shooting lessons Papa gave him and how proud Father was when Will could hit a target the size of a fifty-cent piece at a hundred feet away.

Soon, Mother emerged from the post office, and Will jumped down to help her climb back into the wagon. He didn't mention seeing those two scary men again—no need to frighten her and no need for her to know about the big heavy Colt under his belt.

Will untied the team and headed down the hill on Jefferson Street to the railroad station. The railyard was filled with wagons, carts, and carriages, and crowded with people on the ground, on the docks, and in the station. Many of the men were Union Army soldiers, and there were vendors and traders everywhere. He tied the reins to the wagon and told Mother to stay aboard while he scouted about.

Finally, at the end of the docks, he found the sutlers who were shouting out what they were looking to buy. Some wanted horses and mules, others wanted feed for livestock, and eventually he heard a vendor calling out for food items to feed the army. Will approached him to determine what he was buying. The burly man looked him up and down and asked Will what business it was of his to ask. Will replied that he had potatoes for sale.

"Well, I won't be buying any year-old spuds," the man sneered. "The army does not want them."

"That's not a problem," Will replied. "These were just dug in the past month, and I have twenty-two bushels. I'd prefer to sell to one buyer, not shop all over."

"What do you want for them, sonny?"

Will waited a moment and said he heard the army was paying $1.25 a bushel.

"Well, sonny, I am not the U.S. Army," the man growled. "I sell to them for a profit, and I'll give you seventy-five cents a bushel."

"Thanks," Will said, "but I'll go back up on Main Street where I can get better than a dollar a bushel all day long."

As he turned to walk away, the man called out, "Hey, son, come back here. We are not finished."

Will kept walking back to his wagon, and the man followed him. At the wagon, the sutler said, "What do you mean by turning your back and walking away from me? I ought to thrash you a good one and teach you some manners."

Will squared off on him and pulled back his jacket just enough to show the big Colt .44 in his belt. "You better take your best swing, as it might be your last."

The sutler retreated a step, rubbed his jaw, and said, "Son, I was just testing you a bit. You say you have twenty-two bushels of fresh-dug potatoes? I'll take a look if they are what you say they are. I'll buy your twenty-two bushels for $1.10 a bushel. Cash, of course."

Will did not say a word but grabbed a bushel and pulled the twine off, opened the bag, and dumped half of it at the feet of the sutler.

"Son, those are beautiful spuds, and I'll take them all for a total of twenty-four dollars and twenty cents."

"Done," said Will. "Let's see the money."

As he pocketed the cash in his jacket, Will gave Mother a nod and climbed into the back of the wagon, where he quickly slid all twenty-two bags to the rear tailgate for the sutler. When finished, Will closed the tailgate on the wagon and climbed into the driver's seat.

"Mother, are you ready to go home?"

"Yes," she said, "and you did very well with that ignorant man. I'm so happy you got an extra ten cents a bushel from him."

"Mother, before we go, let me say this: We have a lot of money on us, and I want to make sure we keep it safe. I'm going to put the horse blanket over our knees and put the pistol on the seat beside me and the rifle pointed down between us."

Mother looked at Will with a puzzled look but immediately pulled the blanket in place while Will put the two guns where they would be handy.

Will clucked a bit and slapped the reins lightly, spurring Tom and Queen to go moving. At the top of Jefferson Street, Will turned right and headed north on Main Street toward home. Amazingly, Tom and Queen seemed to sense that they were headed home, and pulling an empty wagon, they began to trot. Will planned to stop at the bottom of Main Street and water them at a public trough and then start the climb up the long hill out of town.

As Will passed Kelly's Tavern, he was alarmed to see Blackie and Buckskin dismount from their horses and tie them to the hitchrack in front of the tavern. Blackie stood beside his magnificent black stallion of about fifteen hands high while Buckskin rested a hand on his nice-looking dun mare.

Both men looked at Will and his wagon, causing Will to feel very uneasy. He dropped his hand to the grip of the big .44 to reassure himself. Mother didn't seem to notice any of this, which pleased Will.

4

Headed Home

The team took in water quickly and then headed up the hill. Once they had reached the flat road at the top, Tom and Queen again broke into a trot and made good time homeward. Soon, they came to the fork in the road where the stagecoaches would continue north to Erie, while Will and the wagon would take the fork to the right to head to West Sunbury.

The sound of hoofbeats drew Will's attention, and he looked back over his shoulder. A cold chill ran down his back as he saw two riders coming from behind and recognized the horses and the riders as Blackie and Buckskin.

I knew it! he thought. *They were tracking me all over town—and still are. Likely intent on robbing us.*

Will heard the gait of the horses behind him increase from a trot to a lope, and he again gripped the Colt pistol. A few seconds later, the riders came alongside Will and his wagon. Expecting the worst, Will was ready for them to try to stop him, but they just pulled alongside and kept up their speed. Blackie went by first, and when Buckskin pulled alongside, he looked over. He tipped his hat at Mother with a small smile on his face. With that, the two riders passed them and rode off ahead of them toward West Sunbury as well.

Will relaxed a bit but couldn't help but wonder what these two were up to and if he'd see them again. He'd never seen them around West Sunbury, and it seemed odd that they would be starting a long ride late in the day. They didn't have bedrolls on their saddles or any extra gear that a rider might have for a longer journey. Will decided not to worry Mother by discussing any of his concerns, but he felt glad they still had plenty of daylight and the team was strong enough to keep up a good pace headed home.

The miles rolled off quickly in the warm November afternoon. Mother seemed at ease and lost in thought, perhaps pondering significant questions . . .

How was her husband doing off at war?

Why was he fighting in a young man's war?

How would she fare this winter with all her youngsters?

Would the feed Will had stored away during the summer last till next summer?

Would the firewood he and Albert cut last month be enough for the winter?

What would President Lincoln do to bring this terrible war to an end?

Mother could not grasp the concept of slavery; how could one human being think they had the right to own another and subjugate the slave to hard labor? She'd never seen a slave and had only once ever seen a Negro when she was much younger. Andrew's first ancestor to America was Andreas Eschenbach, a missionary and preacher for the Moravian Church, the brotherhood of mankind. Members of this denomination believed all were created equal, no matter whether their skin was white or black or brown. They also believed women and men were equal.

Although Andreas had later left the Church, it was not over a dispute on this doctrine but rather one where his congregation had refused to follow Moravian plans for design and architecture. Doctrine called for a two-story significant structure for the church in Bethlehem, Pennsylvania, but the congregation voted for a one-story log building. Andreas railed against his congregation with such fervor that the head of the Moravian Church in Germany wrote to the leaders in Pennsylvania that Andreas should be removed from giving sermons. Appalled, Andreas resigned from the church but taught his thirteen children the doctrine of equality.

Mother assumed the belief in equality had been so engrained in Andrew—even though he was four generations removed from Andreas—that he was fighting in the war to make some small contribution to end slavery. They had never discussed his decision to join the Union Army. He simply told her he had prayed and it was God's will that he go off to fight for this "just and moral cause."

5

Conflict at the Crossing

Will had descended the last hill on the way home. At the bottom was the new railroad line and the pile of rail ties. Just beyond the tracks flowed Muddy Creek, the stream that had been running so high and fast when they crossed the small bridge over it this morning. Tom started neighing, and Queen seemed to be on high alert too. Will thought the new rail crossing caused unease or maybe the smell of creosote on the high stack of rail ties bothered them.

The wagon rattled over the tracks, the iron wheels clanking against the worn wooden beams. Will barely had time to exhale before the sound of pounding hoofbeats thundered from behind. He twisted in his seat just as a lone rider bore down on them.

Blackie.

The outlaw's black stallion tore past in a blur of muscle and dust before he wheeled it around in a tight arc, cutting them off. Blackie's face twisted in a grimace, his left hand clutching a pistol aimed skyward while his right seized Tom's rein.

"Hold up, boy!" Blackie bellowed, jerking back hard. "Hand over the money!"

His stallion pranced wildly, nostrils flaring, nearly colliding with Tom in the chaos. Blackie struggled to keep his balance, his pistol waving erratically as he fought to level it at Will's mother. The horse's agitated movement kept jarring his aim, making it impossible to steady his grip.

Will didn't hesitate. His hand flashed to his holster, fingers curling around the worn grip of his Colt .44. He yanked it free and fired.

The gun's report cracked through the air.

Blackie grunted, his body jolting as the bullet slammed into the left side of his chest. His hold on Tom's rein faltered, and he twisted in the saddle, a strangled shout escaping his lips. His stallion reared in panic, its hooves striking the air.

Still, Blackie clung on, his pistol still raised, his mouth working as if to curse Will and his mother.

Will didn't give him the chance.

He recocked the pistol, steadied his hand, and squeezed the trigger again.

The bullet hit dead center—right in Blackie's forehead.

His eyes went wide, shock freezing his face for an instant before the force of the shot sent him toppling backward. His body tumbled off the horse, landing in a lifeless heap on the dirt road.

Will barely had time to draw a breath before movement in the distance caught his eye.

Buckskin.

The second outlaw burst from behind a stack of railroad ties, his horse galloping at full tilt. He had a rifle in his hands, already trying to fire off wild shots. The first bullet whined past the wagon, the second kicking up dust near Will's boots.

"Mother, get down!" Will shouted, snatching up the Henry rifle from beneath the wagon blanket.

He dropped to one knee, using the wagon seat as a rest, steadying his aim. Buckskin was closing fast, maybe fifty yards now, still firing, his shots missing wildly as his horse jostled beneath him.

Will exhaled, steadied his sights on Buckskin's chest, and squeezed the trigger.

The rifle bucked against his shoulder.

Buckskin jerked in the saddle, his body snapping backward as the bullet struck home. For a moment, it looked like he might fall—but he clung on, wrenching the reins hard and wheeling away. Blood darkened his shirt, but he spurred his horse toward the railroad tracks, desperate to escape.

Will worked the lever, chambering another round.

He fired again. Buckskin's hat flew from his head, spinning through the air, but still, he pressed on.

One more shot.

Will lined up his sights and squeezed the trigger.

This time, Buckskin's horse stumbled, its gait faltering, but it didn't go down. The outlaw hunched low over the saddle, urging the animal up the hill toward Butler, disappearing into the distance.

Will exhaled, lowering the rifle. His pulse thundered in his ears.

The danger had passed—for now.

But he knew Buckskin would be back. And next time, he wouldn't come alone.

⸺⸙⸺

Will reached down and helped Mother back to her seat.

"Are you all right?" he asked. She said she was fine and asked what happened to the second rider. Will described the scene—how the rider had been firing at them, how he fired three shots, and what Will thought happened to the would-be robber.

Mother remained quiet for what seemed like an hour, but it was only minutes till she spoke.

"We need to get rid of the dead man's body," she said solemnly. "We should tie up his horse to the wagon and then get on home."

Will nodded in agreement.

Still shaken by the shocking events of the past minutes, Mother then sat upright and explained what she thought they should do.

"First, search the man's pockets for anything of value and hand it to me. Then cut off all his clothes and stuff them in a potato sack, along with the hat, boots, and anything else. Put the sack in the wagon. Then get your rope and use his horse to drag him several hundred yards downstream. Untie him and roll him into the creek. Bring the horse back and tie him to the back of the wagon and gather up the guns they dropped, pick up all shells, and bring everything to the wagon."

Will, still filled with adrenaline coursing through his body, did as Mother instructed and soon was back in the driver's seat on the wagon. He made the clucking sound to get Tom and Queen moving ahead. They rode in silence for a long while.

Finally, Mother reached over to pat Will's arm and said, "Son, you did the right thing back there. That awful man would have stolen all our money—money we need to live on—and likely killed both of us. And Lord knows what else he and his partner might have done. I can hardly imagine the children at home trying to survive without us there with them."

They rode on in silence for a while longer before Mother spoke again. "When we get home, I want you to tend to the team, put the black horse in a separate stall, and feed him too. Then take some lamp oil and burn the clothes and boots in the bag. You and I will figure out what to do next after all the children are in bed. When you searched his pockets, what did you find?"

Will pulled out a drawstring bag and handed it to Mother. She pulled the strings open and carefully poured the contents onto the wagon seat between them. She counted out over fifty dollars in coins and bills. *My,* she thought, *this man has been up to a lot of no good to have this much money.*

It seemed like they had been on the road for days instead of hours, but soon the team turned into the driveway to home. Will stopped in front of the house, helped Mother off the wagon, and handed her the bag of shopping goods. She quickly went to the front door as the young ones came bursting out of the house to greet her. Will clucked to the team, and they headed to the barn, where he backed the wagon into the shed. He unhitched the horses, pulled off their harnesses, and hung the sets on their pegs. Both horses drank deeply from the water trough before Will led them to their stalls, where they would be given an extra helping of oats and hay. Albert had already tended to the young team and the cows and, much to Will's surprise, had done the evening milking and poured the milk into the cooling jug in the spring house.

Will went to the toolshed and got a pint of lamp oil and a match. He walked behind the barn where those in the house wouldn't see him and grabbed the foul-smelling bag of Blackie's filthy clothes. Will picked up the bearskin coat but decided he wouldn't burn it, at least not right now, so he put it with the horse blankets in the stable. It seemed too valuable and useful to see it go up in smoke. He dumped the clothes out of the potato sack, checked the pockets one more time, poured the lamp oil all over them, and struck the match.

In minutes, Will had a good fire going. He went back to the toolshed, grabbed an iron rod, and came back to the fire. The iron rod was useful in stirring the fire to make sure everything burned. The leather boots and the soles were the slowest to ignite, but eventually they burned steadily, and Will made sure he turned them over until nothing but ash was left. In the light of the fire, he raked out the few metal buttons and a handful of nails that had been in the boot heels. He waited until the metal had cooled and then picked them up.

Darkness had fallen, and Will made his way back to the house as the bright moon came over the top of the hill to the east. Mother was waiting with a hot slice of ham and browned potatoes sitting on the kitchen table. Albert excitedly asked to hear about the trip. Will felt exhausted but wanted to please his brother. So he gave a detailed account of how well Tom and Queen performed, how well the sales went at each of the establishments, how beautiful the weather had been, and most of all how much he'd enjoyed the day with Mother.

Will asked Albert about his day, and Albert proudly reported that he'd done all the evening chores, including milking Betsy all by himself. Albert said the younger ones had been well behaved except for Priscilla, the youngest, who whined and cried that she missed her mother. Albert said they had sat at the kitchen table at noon, and he served the ham, homemade bread, and jam Mother had prepared, and they were delighted.

"Will," Albert said when he'd finished his report, "you didn't say anything about the black horse that's in the barn. Where did he come from?"

Will responded with a half-truth that he'd found the horse along the road and the rider wasn't around, so Will tied the horse to the wagon and brought it home. Satisfied with the explanation, Albert headed upstairs, and Mother motioned to Will to stay behind.

"Will, I've been thinking," she said when she was sure Albert was out of earshot. "The other man may have been so badly wounded that he didn't survive. But likely he'd be found along the road with a gunshot wound or two. On the other hand, if he survived, he'd probably ride back into Butler and could summon the sheriff to report he'd been shot. In that case, he'd say that his partner had also been shot. He could describe exactly where, as it was right at the railroad tracks on the West Sunbury Road. He could also tell what stores he'd seen you deliver the potatoes, and Mr. Kelly or Mr. Thompson would remember our last name. So, it wouldn't take much investigation to bring the sheriff here looking for you, possibly as a suspected murderer."

She paused to let all that sink in for Will and then continued. "I've been thinking what to do, and I want you to take the black horse and ride out early tomorrow morning to Kittanning in Armstrong County and find the McNabb family. My family, the Dixons, came over from Ireland with the McNabbs. Their son William married a woman named Laura. He has been off to the war since it began, and she is there with their three children, two girls named Laura and Sara and the baby boy named Bill. I want you to lie low there, and I will write to Laura once I know more here about the situation."

Will felt stunned at the idea of leaving home for the unknown. "Mother, I would worry about you and the children if I left, although I know Albert is a capable helper. I'd hate to go, but I think you're right. It's too risky for me to stay here, especially with the horse in the barn. Your plan makes sense."

They talked in hushed tones for a few more minutes, and then Will began preparing for his morning journey. He decided that he'd take the bearskin coat because winter was coming, and he'd need it. In his room, he gathered a clean shirt, trousers, long underwear, and a wool blanket, rolling it into a bedroll. He put all these items by the door, knowing he'd leave well before dawn. He decided he would not say good-bye to the youngsters so he wouldn't have to explain where he was going and why.

6

Ride Away

Will slipped out of bed about five a.m. and pulled on his clothes. With a heavy heart, he quietly stepped into the hallway and past the bedroom doors where his siblings slept and past Mother's door. As he found his way downstairs in the dark, he wondered if he would ever see any of them again or ever sleep in the house where he had been born. To his surprise, he found Mother seated at the kitchen table, the lamp turned down low, and a small fire burning in the kitchen stove. Will could tell she had been crying and guessed she had been up all night.

"Will, here is the plan," she said in a voice slightly above a whisper. "Ride the black horse over to North Washington, and from there the road goes east and down to the river at Parkers Landing. This is the Allegheny River, and it flows all the way south to Pittsburgh. I don't know if the construction is finished on a bridge over the river, but if not, there should be a ferry crossing where a man will pull his raft with you for a fee. Once on the other side, a road follows the river, and you will come to the town of Kittanning. The McNabb house is on Oak Street near Main Street, and just ask for them since they are well-known. I've written a letter to take with you introducing you to Mrs. McNabb. She will take you in, and I will write to her as soon as I can and fill her in on what I know here."

Will quickly finished his breakfast of two eggs, homemade bread, and coffee. Mother handed him a small cloth sack and said she had prepared three boiled eggs, three ham slices, and some bread for his trip. She hugged him, and Will was filled with remorse of maybe seeing his mother for the last time, or for at least a long time.

Hugging her tight, Will whispered, "I love you, Mother." And as they both wiped away tears, he said, "Please hug all the young ones for me."

With that, he pulled on his coat, boots, and hat and headed for the barn.

Albert would now be in charge, but Will fed the horses and cows one last time. While the black horse ate, Will filled three bags of oats to take care of the horse for the ride. He curried out the horse, brushed down the coat, and picked each hoof to make sure there were no small stones in the hoof. Many times, he had heard his father's words, "Take care of your horse and your horse will take care of you." Will grabbed another small sack and stashed away a brush and curry comb, and decided he could use his jackknife to clean the hoofs in the future. With that, the black horse was finished eating, so Will saddled him, slipped on the headstall, and easily placed the bit between the horse's teeth. Will used the lead rope to help securely tie the bedroll. Blackie had a nice pair of saddlebags behind the saddle that Will used to securely stow the bags of oats, feed, and tools.

Will led the black horse out of the stable and paused by the wagon shed to retrieve the bearskin coat. He slipped it over the saddle and mounted up. He did not want Mother to see that he had not burned the coat.

⚮

In the crisp morning, the bright moonlight helped him find his way. He had hunted deer as far away as North Washington, probably seven miles as the crow flies. Will decided it might be better just to ride cross-country and not attract any attention in West Sunbury. The black horse sensed the excitement of heading off on a trip and, in the cold light of dawn, quickly struck a trot. It seemed like no time before he reached the road leading into North Washington.

Will was surprised to see several riders, wagons, and carriages traveling north at the crossroads. He waited for a few to pass, then rode on to the east toward Parkers Landing. The horse wanted to lope, and the road was frozen hard, so it seemed safe to let him have his way for a bit. Will was pleased at how smooth a gait the black horse had, and they covered a lot of ground in the next hour.

For the next two hours, the pace was a walk, and soon they were at the top of a steep hill descending to Parkers Landing and the river. River Road was filled with wagons, carriages, riders, and walkers. All seemed to be headed north as well. Will finally saw a walker resting on a rock and asked him what all the excitement was about.

"Oil," shouted the walker. "A new field has been discovered just north of here, and everyone wants to find work or stake a claim."

Will could not grasp what oil meant, how it was found, what it would be used for, or why so many were rushing to the fields.

Mother had given him ten dollars to help with his travels, so he rode over to the ferry boat dock. He could see the raft and the rope that connected it between the shores. A stout, dirty-looking man would pull hard on the rope and move the raft across the river. When he arrived, he unloaded six men who must all have been struck with the oil fever as well, since they hurried off the boat and headed to the general store across the street.

"Sonny, are you crossing the river or just taking up space on my dock?" growled the ferryman.

Will was taken aback by his gruff manner but simply asked the cost to transport him and his horse.

"One dollar," the man sneered.

When Will responded that a dollar seemed like a lot of money for such a short ride, the man said, "You and your horse can swim across for free if you would like."

Will dug out a dollar bill, handed it to the man, and led his horse to the raft. Once loaded, the ferryman cast off the rope and started the trip back across the river. Will broke the silence by asking about the oil field workers.

"I been busy from dawn to dark hauling men and equipment from the east bank to Parkers Landing for over a week, ever since the well struck oil a mile north." He added with a grin, "That's why I can charge a dollar per crossing. These days, that price is a bargain."

"I don't understand the excitement about oil," Will admitted.

"This kind of oil will replace whale oil for lamps," the man explained. "Plus, the army needs it for the war, although I don't know why."

Once they docked, Will led the horse up to the road and headed south. The road followed the river, and Will kept meeting one man after another all headed north to the oil fields. They were a hard-looking lot, causing Will to wonder if someone might try to rob him and take his black horse. He pulled the .44 from a saddlebag and tucked it into his waistband.

There were migrant camps along the road, which looked seedy and sketchy to Will. He began to worry about where he'd spend the night, as these November days were growing shorter on daylight. As he rounded a bend in the road, he came across a farmer whose wagon was stuck in a hole at the road's edge. Will asked the driver if he could give him a hand.

"Be much obliged if you would," said the farmer.

First, Will helped dig around the front of the stuck wheel and then tried to add his weight and muscle to push on the wagon as the farmer urged his team forward. The wagon rocked a bit and seemed to almost break free, but not quite enough to get unstuck.

Will noticed the farmer had a rope across his load. He suggested he tie the rope to his saddle and to the tongue of the wagon, then give the team a pull. Doing so proved to be just enough extra force to free the wagon. Will undid the rope, brought it back to the wagon, threw it across the load, and retied it.

The farmer looked down from the wagon and said, "Son, I'm in debt to you, as I don't know how I would have gotten out of that fix without your help. What do I owe you?"

"Nothing, sir. Just glad I came along when I did," Will replied.

Will asked how far he had to go, and the farmer said he lived about a mile south. When Will then asked how far it was to Kittanning, the man said it was at least four hours on a good horse like the one Will was riding.

Will thought for a moment and said, "There is something you could do for me. Could my horse and I sleep in your barn for the night? It does not seem safe out here along this road with all the men headed north."

"Son, that would be just fine. We have a large family and no extra beds, but the barn will do just fine for a night. I'll have my wife feed you a nice hot supper as well. My name is Hoyt Painter, and what is yours?"

"Will Eshenbaugh," he answered. "Thank you, Mr. Painter, that would be very much appreciated."

Soon, they came to the lane leading to the Painter property. Mr. Painter showed Will a stall for the horse. While Will unsaddled and brushed down his horse, Mr. Painter hung the harnesses for his team and turned them into their stalls, feeding them grain and hay. Will fed his horse a quart of oats, and Mr. Painter threw a pitchfork full of hay to Will's horse as well.

After introductions in the house, Mr. Painter announced that Will would be staying for supper and then sleep in the barn for the night. Will looked around the room and counted nine children, who each looked to be about a year apart in age. Soon, Mrs. Painter had them all seated and found a stool for Will at one corner of the table. When Mr. Painter bowed his head, everyone, including Will, did the same. Mr. Painter said a long and thankful grace. Mrs. Painter then ladled out huge bowls of potato soup with pieces of ham. They all ate in silence, and soon Will said he'd head for the barn, thanking the farmer and his wife once again for the place to spend the night.

⁂

By dawn, Will was up, had fed the horse, eaten a piece of ham Mother had packed, and led the horse out of the barn. As he mounted up, he heard Mr. Painter from the porch of the house call out to him. Will rode over to the yard and bid Mr. Painter good morning.

"Mrs. Painter is going to be very disappointed if you ride off without a good breakfast," the man said. "Please come join us."

Will tied the horse to a hitching post and followed Mr. Painter into the house. He immediately breathed deeply, savoring the wonderful smell of bacon frying in a large black skillet on the cookstove next to a griddle of pancakes. With the children still asleep, it was just Mr. and Mrs. Painter and Will at the table. It did not take long to polish off a stack of pancakes and slices of thick-cut bacon.

"Thank you for the two delicious meals and the safe place to sleep," Will said. "Now I will get on with my journey and let you get on with your day."

He donned the bearskin coat against the cold November morning, glad he had that coat to pull over him last night as he slept on the pile of hay in the barn.

The horse was full of energy again this morning and quickly broke into a trot south along the river. On the horizon appeared a large smokestack and a noisy building under the stack. As Will approached, he tried to figure out what exactly he was looking at. This strange apparatus appeared to be on the water. As he watched, Will realized it was moving toward him and was belching smoke from the stack and had a large wheel on the side that appeared to be moving the apparatus upriver.

He stared in wonder for a long time until a traveler on the road came along.

"Excuse me, sir," Will called out, pointing toward the water. "Can you tell me what I'm looking at there?"

The fellow gave a snort and said, "What's the matter with you, boy? You never seen a steamboat before?"

"No, I haven't, sir." He suddenly realized that he'd spent his sixteen years on the farm and there were probably many things he hadn't seen.

Will guessed that the steamboat must also be filled with oil field workers headed north. He could not imagine where all these men were coming from and why they were not off at the war like all the men Will knew.

Will turned south again with his horse trotting along at a steady pace. His thoughts turned to the events of the past few days, and he wondered if Mother was coping well, if the sheriff had come snooping around, and if Buckskin had survived and where he might be if he was alive.

7

A Warm Welcome

Before he realized it, Will had ridden into the town of Kittanning. He slowed the horse to a walk and rode down Main Street. He knew from Mother that the McNabbs lived on a side street, but he was not sure where. He decided the best place to find out was the post office, and he soon found it across from a general store.

Entering the building, Will approached an elderly man behind the counter who sized him up without saying anything. Will asked if he could be directed to the McNabb house.

"What business is it of yours where the McNabbs live?" the postmaster responded curtly.

Will explained that he was passing through, and the McNabbs were related on his mother's side.

Apparently satisfied, the old man said, "Go down Main Street two blocks, then turn left. The house is the second one on the right."

Will tipped his hat in appreciation and outside remounted the horse and followed the directions to the McNabb house. Arriving, he tied the horse to the hitching rail and walked to the front door. After knocking once, the door opened slightly, and a woman asked who he was. Will answered, and the door flew open as Mrs. McNabb rushed out to greet him.

"Oh, young man, I am so surprised and delighted to see anyone from the Dixon family!" she practically squealed.

"My middle name is Dixon," Will said, "honoring my mother's side of the family."

Mrs. McNabb asked Will what in the world brought him this way.

"Well, ma'am, there were some troubles back home, and my mother wrote a letter to deliver to you by way of introduction." He fetched it from his jacket pocket and handed it over.

"By all means, come inside and tell me all about your ride here."

Once inside, Mrs. McNabb brought Will a glass of water and motioned for him to take a seat at the kitchen table. Will told her about all the men headed north, the steamboat on the river, and the night spent in the farmer's barn.

Mrs. McNabb said that he was welcome in her home, and she would like to read the letter. She instructed Will to take his horse around back to the stable, unsaddle it, and feed him while she read the letter.

When Will returned to the kitchen, Mrs. McNabb said she would do anything she could to help and that Mother asked if Will could stay with the McNabbs until she could figure out the next steps. She showed Will a cot on the rear porch where he was welcome to sleep.

Apparently, the sound of their voices awakened the three youngsters, and soon Laura, Sara, and little Billy were surrounding their mother in the kitchen, curious about this stranger in their home. Mrs. McNabb told the children of her friendship with Will's mother, Mary Ann, and about the time his father, Andrew, had visited right before the start of the war.

Turning to Will, she explained that her husband, William P. McNabb, had insisted that he and his brother had a duty to enlist and serve in the Union, even though they had families and were in their late twenties. So, in August 1861, both had enlisted for a three-year hitch.

Laura recounted stories Mr. McNabb had shared last winter when he was home on leave. He had told bits and pieces of the gruesome battle at Antietam, Maryland, in the fall of 1862. Then last summer, he wrote of the horrific three-day fight at Gettysburg and how fortunate he had been to leave the battlefield unharmed while scores of his comrades were either killed or badly wounded.

Mrs. McNabb mentioned that Andrew, then about thirty-six years old, also thought it was his duty to enlist. Shortly thereafter, Andrew was offered three hundred dollars by Phillip Cannon, a wealthy landowner, to take Cannon's place in the army draft to serve a one-year enlistment. Andrew accepted the money, telling his wife that he wanted to leave her with ample money if he was killed or injured, pointing out that army pay of twelve dollars a month would not go far compared to the three hundred dollars he'd received. Mary Ann knew there was no room for further discussion.

Returning to the present situation, Mrs. McNabb said to Will, "It could be several days or longer to receive another letter from your mother. With so many men off at war and the post office not paying much, employees are hard to come by. Mail delivery is not very timely."

"I understand," Will replied. "I am not used to sitting idle, since there is never-ending work on the farm. So I will be happy to help in any way during my stay here, doing chores and making repairs. This afternoon, I believe I will take a walk around town to see my new surroundings."

⸺◦∞◦⸺

Later, as Will strolled the streets of the town, it seemed that most of the businesses were looking to hire workers, as the war and the oil fields had taken so many men away from local jobs. As he walked past the livery barn, the stableman said, "Hey, boy, you looking for work? I could use a strong lad to shovel all the horse manure and fix the stalls. You could sleep here, too, and I'll pay fifty cents a day, seven days a week."

"No thanks," Will replied. "I have a place to stay."

Down along the river, Will heard a high-pitched sound he had not heard before. As he walked farther, he could see large tree trunks that had been cut into lengths being fed into a machine that sliced off boards on each pass through. As he watched, a stranger beside him said, "Is that not something to behold? A steam engine right here in Armstrong County, running a sawmill and cutting more boards in a day than a good man could split in a year."

The stranger moved on, and Will watched in fascination, trying to comprehend how steam could propel the saw blade and the feeder that ran logs along a track and how each board seemed cut to a uniform thickness. He observed how workmen quickly took each newly sawn board and carried it to the river-bank, where it was stacked with other boards. There, more workers were assembling the boards into what looked like a large raft right along the water's edge.

As Will stood there in amazement, the mill shut down after a whistle was blown on the steam engine. The workers all gathered around a rough-sawn table and opened their sacks for the noontime meal. Halfway through the lunch break, a large man looked over at Will, who was sitting on a nearby hill. The man approached Will and asked if he was looking for work.

"I could be," Will said. "It depends on what the work is and how much it pays."

"I'm the boss here, and we are hiring, but only able-bodied men who could work twelve hours a day, six days a week. Son, I have a lot of orders to fill and, what with the war and now the oil fever, not nearly enough help around. I could pay you fifty cents a day here."

"Thanks," Will replied, "but I've already been offered that much just to muck stalls, plus a place to sleep each night. I might consider a dollar per day for the twelve hours of hard labor and six days a week as well."

"That's what I'm paying the most skilled man on the job," the boss protested. "I could pay you eighty cents a day, but you'd need to start today. I pay every Saturday night at the end of the day, but you'd better decide now since I need to get this crew back to work."

"I'll take it," Will said. "And you won't regret it. Tell me what to do to get started."

8

New Life in Kittanning

Bossman introduced Will to the crew at the far end of the saw blade. Then Will was shown the simple task of grabbing newly sawn boards and taking them to the stack by the river. The work was hard and the pace relentless as one board after another was sheared from a log, and the noise of the saw blade whine was never-ending and piercing.

Finally, at dark, the whistle blew, and the shift was finished. Will asked the boss what time they started tomorrow, and the answer was daybreak. Will walked back to the McNabb house, thrilled that he had earned six hours' pay of forty cents for his first shift and could make $4.80 a week starting tomorrow. He contrasted that to all the men off at war where privates made only twelve dollars a month.

Will was excited to report his good fortunes to Mrs. McNabb, but she was upset that Will had been gone all day without any word from him. She had worried that some harm had befallen him. He explained his new job and the pay, but Mrs. McNabb seemed even more worried. She shared with Will that she had heard that several men had been badly injured at the mill and maybe one or two fatally lost to the whirling blade, the high-speed belts, and rolling logs. One man, she said, had fallen overboard off a raft and drowned. Will promised her he would be extra careful and watch that none of his clothing was loose to avoid being pulled into a horrible maiming or even death.

The next day at their noontime meal break, Will asked one of the workers what would happen to the raft they were building with the sawn boards.

"Lad, they are floated down to Pittsburgh, and the lumber is sold to the highest bidder," the man explained. "With all the war production of iron, there's a huge demand for the lumber for houses and even planks for road cover to get wagons through muddy places."

He went on to add that the rafts were loaded with barrels of cabbages and grain and piled high with hay, all of which were sold in Pittsburgh. The rafts had a crew of three men who ran the raft ashore each evening, camped, and slept onboard. Once they had sold everything in Pittsburgh, the men would walk back to Kittanning, where they would be paid in full for the trip. Generally, the head of the crew was the businessman who took the risk of buying the lumber and navigating the raft to Pittsburgh, selling his goods, and returning home. He wanted the crew with him on the way home to help protect against getting robbed.

At the end of Saturday's workday, the boss told Will he'd done a good job and handed him $3.60, pay for four and a half days of work. Will had never possessed so much money of his own and, other than the potato sales' money in Butler, had never seen so much money. When he got back to the McNabb house, he went around back and washed up at the pump, cold as it was. He was covered in sawdust and sweat from the hard week of labor.

When he walked into the house, Mrs. McNabb had a meal prepared of a pig roast, potatoes, carrots, and onions along with freshly made bread and strawberry jam. Will was grateful for a warm house, a tasty dinner, and a day off tomorrow.

Mrs. McNabb said she had a couple of surprises for Will. She had taken his clothes and underwear and washed them and dried them on the clothesline out back in the warm afternoon sun.

"I also carried in two buckets of water, now heating on the stove," she said. "You're welcome to fill the big tub I dragged in and used to bathe all the youngsters earlier. Feel free to use it right after I retire for the night."

"Sounds wonderful," he said. "I'm used to getting plenty dirty from farm work, but a sawmill kicks up dirt and dust of a whole different kind."

"A favor to ask of you, Will," she said. "Would you be able to accompany me and the children to church tomorrow morning?"

He said of course he would be glad to, and then he rummaged in his pocket and pulled out two dollars. Handing it to her, he said, "For food and lodging and other kindnesses you're providing."

Mrs. McNabb looked shocked and refused the money. But when Will explained how much the sawmill was paying him, she relented and received the two dollars with gratitude.

After taking a bath and scrubbing the sawdust out of his hair and ears and everywhere sawdust could get, Will dried and dressed in clean clothes, feeling like a new man. He emptied the bathwater into the buckets and carried them outside. Back in the house, he took another dollar bill and tucked it into a side pocket on his saddlebags. He thought of Mother and how surprised she would be when she received a letter from him with money enclosed.

<hr>

One day at lunch break the next week, Will asked Bossman how much he paid a man to go downriver with him.

"Same wages," he answered, "but only for three days. If it takes longer, the workers aren't paid anything more."

Will asked what he charged to haul a horse downriver.

"Normally three dollars," the boss explained. "But if you want to work as a hand, you and a horse could go at half your wages. I'm leaving in a couple of days and already have a full crew and load. But in two or three weeks, I'll be ready for another run, right after Christmas."

The boss added that once the winter snows and rains started, usually in January, the river might get too high and the currents too strong to make more trips.

That night, Will lay awake trying to figure out what to do next. He hoped he would hear from Mother soon about any news on the sheriff and any possible investigation into Blackie's death. Until he heard from her, he planned to lie low at the McNabb house and keep working at the mill.

Two weeks later, much to Will's relief, Mother's letter to Mrs. McNabb arrived. Inside was an envelope addressed to Will. He anxiously opened it and read the news from home. First, she reported that everything was well at the farm and that Albert was handling all the chores just fine. He had even started working the young team some. Then she reported that the sheriff had come by the house. He said a badly shot-up fellow had come to Butler and reported that he and his partner had been ambushed near the railroad tracks south of West Sunbury. The wounded man said he was lucky to have escaped with his life but feared his partner was not so fortunate. He described him as stocky and breaded, dressed in black, and riding a black stallion. Mother described what happened next:

The sheriff asked if he could look around the stable and buildings, and of course I gave him permission. When he came back to the house, he accepted an offer of hot coffee and freshly baked apple pie. He shared that he suspected the shot-up man and the missing man of having committed several robberies. They seemed to be on the lookout along Main Street for anyone selling goods or unsuspecting travelers they could rob.

The sheriff said without a body, he could not arrest anyone for murder, and as far as he could tell, he was not going to spend more time trying to find who had shot the man in buckskin clothes. He added that the world would probably be a better place if the man in buckskin had been mortally wounded and added further that there had been an end to the robberies of travelers since the shooting.

Will, you might want to get rid of the black horse and anything else that could offer a clue about the shootings, even if that means walking back home when the time comes.

Will tossed and turned most of the night, pondering Mother's letter and her plans for him to return home. Her plan seemed rational indeed, but he had been planning his own strategy each night as we lay awake wondering where his life would take him. Will was fascinated with the war. What drew Father and his brothers William A., Albert, Joseph, John, and Thomas, along with William McNabb, his brother, and so many more to enlist and go off to battle? Some said it was to preserve the Union against the breakaway by the Confederates, while others said it was to free the Negro slaves. Will was not even sure why those close to him had gone off to war since they had never discussed it within earshot of his young ears.

He crafted a plan to join the next raft to Pittsburgh and take the black horse with him. Once there, he planned to leave the crew, an act that would infuriate the boss and likely mean he would not pay Will for the wages of traveling to Pittsburgh. He wrote a letter to Mrs. McNabb thanking her for taking him in and telling her how much he had enjoyed the time with her, Laura, Sara, and Billy in the evenings and on Sundays after church. He slipped five dollars into the envelope to help her with household expenses.

Will also wrote a letter to Mother telling her he had decided to ride a raft to Pittsburgh and there he would sign up for the army, hopefully in the 14th Pennsylvania Cavalry with his father. He would let her know when he could and put ten dollars in her envelope. He said the war had to come to an end soon and he recalled the teachings of his first ancestor to America, Andreas Eschenbach, the Moravian Church missionary who spread the gospel that all humans were created equal, men and women, whites and blacks. While the family had long ago left the Moravian Church, Will couldn't get away from the concept that Confederates owned and traded slaves and treated them as property. It seemed so inherently wrong that Will had decided it was his time to serve the Union and help abolish slavery.

Before he left, Will rode the black horse into the hills above town and found a nice fir tree, about five feet tall, and used a hatchet from the wagon shed to cut it down. Dragging the tree back to the house, Will found two small boards and a few iron nails and soon had a stand attached to the bottom of the tree. He shook it hard to get all the snow off the branches and carried it into the back of the house, where he stood it up near the front window.

Will called the children, who came running to see what was so exciting, and right behind them came Mrs. McNabb. Of the children, only Laura, the oldest, had ever seen a Christmas tree, as their father had been off to war. Mrs. McNabb said she could pop some popcorn and they could string it around the tree, but she cautioned Will that she was afraid of putting candles on the tree for fear of fire. Will suggested they could light candles and just hold them and maybe sing a song or two that they sang in church.

As they strung the popcorn onto thread, Sara came and sat beside Will. She was almost four and looked at the beauty of the green tree and took Will's hand into her little hand and said, "This is the most wonderful thing I've ever seen!"

9

Down the River

The morning after Christmas, Will slipped out of bed and dressed quickly. He rolled all his clothes into a sack, grabbed his pistol and rifle, placed the two letters on the kitchen table, and headed for the stable. After feeding the black horse, Will quickly saddled him, threw the bearskin coat over the saddle, placed the rifle in the scabbard and the pistol in his belt. He rode out and down to the wharf. Bossman planned to leave first thing that morning for a float to Pittsburgh, and Will had agreed to go along, taking the black horse with him.

The other helper arrived shortly, and Will loaded the black horse onto the raft and tied him off. Bossman shouted at them to push hard to shove the raft away from the dock, and he took the rudder to get them righted and headed downriver. The wind was low, but the morning was cold, and the skies were cloudy. Bossman said he sure hoped it did not rain, as that would make for a cold, miserable trip. Soon, they caught the swift part of the current of the Allegheny River and were moving right along. The raft had a big rudder on the rear to guide it and a big oar on either side for the crew members to help maneuver the raft, especially when coming to shore or dock.

As the day wore on, the weather cleared, and the sun warmed up the raft crew. Will was amazed at the hills on both sides of the river and how many trees covered them. Occasionally, the raft would pass a farm and sometimes a small village with a dock or landing. Often, someone on shore would wave at the raft crew, and Will always waved back.

Late in the afternoon, Bossman called both helpers to the back of the raft. He explained that they would soon make their landfall, a clearing on the river with a sandbar where they could run the front of the raft aground and quickly take the big rope coiled on the front and run ashore to tie off on a mooring post. The two helpers would first use their oars to slow the raft, and when instructed by Bossman, Will was to grab the rope and leap onto land to secure the tie-off. Everything went smoothly, and soon Will had them tied and secured for the night. Will led the black horse off the raft so it could graze on the remaining summer grass along the riverbank.

Bossman built a small fire and made a pot of coffee. He put a skillet on the fire and put a slice of ham on to fry along with a potato he cut up with his pocketknife. When cooked, the ham was cut into three pieces, with each piece placed on a slice of bread.

"Boys," he said, "you'll need to help yourself to the potatoes right out of the skillet."

After eating, Will checked on the black horse and tied him close but where he could graze for the night. On deck, Will found a spot on the side away from the wind and wrapped up tightly in the bearskin coat and fell quickly asleep, lulled by the lapping of small waves against the raft.

Next morning before dawn, Bossman hollered for his two crew members to get up and moving. He handed each of them a cold biscuit and a tin cup of coffee. A moment later, he barked at Will to get his horse onboard the raft. He then had Will and the other helper untie the raft and push it off the sandbar.

Bossman turned the raft to the center of the river and shouted at the crew to row hard so he could then turn and run south with the current. He alerted the crew to keep an eye out for any steamships coming upriver as they did not move for the rafts coming downstream. The day was clear, and they sailed right along with no problems. Twice, they met steamers headed north, but now the river was wide enough that they could pass without issues.

At midday, Bossman broke out two more biscuits and small slices of ham, giving a helping to Will and the other deckhand. Will leaned over the edge and took a drink of water, but it was muddy and had a bad aftertaste. Bossman said he would not drink that river water—too much was being dumped into the river all along its course.

The afternoon went smoothly, but Bossman called both mates to the helm.

"Tonight we will be tying up to a pier, and there will be crew on the pier who will grab the rope," he said. "I will swing the raft around facing upstream to slow it. We do not get any second chances. Understand?" He pointed a finger at Will and added, "So you need to be ready with the up-front line."

Soon, the pier came into sight along with a village behind it. Smoke curled from the chimneys of the houses and the tavern on the dock. As the raft came about, a stout young man shouted to Will to toss the line. Surprisingly, the dockhand missed the toss, but Will quickly recovered the line, and this time the toss was caught, and they were secured for the night.

Will led the black horse ashore and cleaned off the manure from the deck. After feeding the horse his bag of oats, Will led him to a grassy area along the river and picketed him for the night.

Bossman said the tavern offered good meals, and he was going to have a beer or two as well. Will and the other crewman decided to have a hot meal and were served a thick beef stew and freshly baked bread. Will decided to order a beer, although he had never tasted one and his home never had alcohol in it.

While Will sipped on the mug, he decided that either this was not very good beer or beer took a lot of getting used to. Either way, he was not in a hurry to try beer again anytime soon.

He and the mate walked back to the raft, and Will checked the tie line for the black horse. Will decided to tie extra knots into both ends of the rope to make it that much harder for anyone to try to steal the horse during the night. For extra precaution, Will decided to sleep on the side of the raft facing the horse and tucked the pistol into his waistband.

Asleep just a few minutes, Will was jolted awake by a loud ruckus on the dockside. He jumped up and pulled his pistol in case he needed it. The commotion turned out to be Bossman trying to stand up and walk onto the boat. Will had never seen anyone with too much to drink, but that seemed to be the obvious reason for the noise and cursing from Bossman. Once Bossman settled down, he fell into a deep sleep and snored almost immediately.

Just about the time Will fell asleep again, he heard the black horse whinny and stomp his feet. Will jumped up and ran toward the horse, his .44 pistol in hand. Sure enough, two slim men were trying to untie the knots and make off with Will's horse. He fired a shot in the air, and the two scoundrels ran back past the tavern. No one else seemed to mind a shot fired late at night, to Will's surprise. He decided the best plan was to load the black horse back on the raft and put himself between the horse and the dock.

⸎

Without offering any breakfast, Bossman told the boys, with shouts and curses, to cast off. He'd get them to the middle of the river in the dark. For the first time on the river, Will felt frightened. Was Bossman still drunk? Why was he so gruff, and did he have any idea how to run the raft in the dark? Fortunately, they seemed to drift along, and slowly dawn broke over the hills to the east.

"Boys, we should make Pittsburgh today, probably well before sundown!" Bossman yelled. "I told you we might be able to do it in three days."

Late in the morning, Bossman called the lads to the back of the raft. He said he'd plumb forgotten about anything to eat this morning and again shared biscuits and cold ham from his sack. Will watched the banks of the river and saw more and more houses along the shoreline. Many more steamboats were headed north, some loaded with men and some with barrels, crates, and livestock. Will figured this oil work was far bigger than he had originally understood.

As the day wore on, the buildings that now lined the shores were sometimes more than two stories, and some were built of stone or brick. They floated past an island, and suddenly the stench hit them, so bad it made Will wretch. He made his way to the back and asked Bossman what in the world had they passed.

"Herr's Island," Bossman said with a booming laugh. "A slaughterhouse where mostly hogs and cattle are butchered. Got to feed the growing number of people in town, you know. It's a perfect location for the slaughterhouse. They just dump all the unused parts of the animals into the river."

Will made another note to himself to never drink river water ever again.

Mid-afternoon, Bossman called them together. "Boys, we are almost to our landing. This time, I will bring the raft around to point straight to shore and run it into the shore as far as it will go. Will, as soon as you can, jump off with the rope and tie it to one of the trees or mooring posts and make it snug."

In fifteen minutes, Will could feel the raft turn and head straight into land. He positioned himself at the front, and the second he saw land under the raft he jumped down and tugged the heavy rope up the slope to a large post, snubbing off the raft. Almost immediately, a group of men descended on the raft, wanting to know what was for sale. Bossman came to the front of the raft and greeted a few of them by name.

"I'm going to sell one item at a time," Bossman shouted, "so let me hear your bids and see your cash. No Confederate money accepted here."

First, he sold a barrel of cabbages, then two barrels of apples, each to the highest bidder. After selling the hams, bacon slabs, and the rest of the cargo, he offered to sell the stack of hay. He told the bidders the hay would have to be removed today as he planned to sell the wooden raft in the morning. Someone called out a bid of five dollars for the black horse and saddle, and Will quickly let it be known that the horse and rig were not for sale.

Turns out, the hay was bought by the owner of the local stable, and he was back in an hour with two laborers along with his team and wagon. They made short order of pitching the hay onto the wagon. While they waited, Will asked where the stable was located and how much it would cost to board his horse there. The stableman said it was twenty-five cents a night for a stall and hay and thirty cents if the owner wanted to sleep in the same stall. That seemed odd, so Will asked him why an owner would sleep in the stall.

"Son, if you want your horse to be there in the morning, you might want to sleep beside it," the man said. "The army is buying up all the horses and mules they can get, so thieves steal them at night and sell them to army buyers the next morning."

Will asked Bossman if he could sleep on the raft that night, and Bossman said he'd be glad to have the company. But he warned Will to keep his pistol and rifle handy as a lot of men had seen Bossman sell his cargo today and might come sneaking around that night to try to rob him.

The other crewman asked for his pay, and Bossman paid him off, and the fellow jumped ashore and headed to a tavern across the wharf. Bossman reminded Will of their deal that Will's pay would cover the cost of having the black horse taking up space on the raft.

Bossman told Will he had done a good job as a novice raftsman and invited him to share a supper of fried ham and potatoes. Will agreed, grateful for the hot meal.

During dinner, Bossman asked, "So, son, what are your plans now?"

"I am going to the army recruiting office and see if I can sign up for the cavalry," Will explained.

Bossman listened and finally said, "I hear the army will let you bring your own horse and will pay you monthly for it if the horse and you are able to serve. But they will not let you bring your saddle and tack or your rifle and pistol since you will be issued new ones. If you enlist, I am willing to buy the saddle, tack, and guns from you for ten dollars."

Will had not thought about those issues, but they made sense. "I'll sleep on it and let you know."

⸺ ⚬⚬⚬ ⸺

In the morning, Will decided he would need to sell, but he also was not willing to walk around Pittsburgh without at least his pistol on him. He told Bossman they would have a deal if the army accepted him today, but he would need to keep the pistol. They shook hands, and Will said he hoped to be back by noon. Bossman said that would be fine as he hoped to have the lumber from the raft sold by then.

Will led the black horse behind him and walked up across the docks to the first street. He saw a group of men in uniforms and asked if they might know where the army recruiting office might be located. One of them scoffed and said, "Sonny, all of us wish we had never found it, so take my advice and go back to your farm and stay there until this war is over."

Will walked away puzzled by the response but remained undeterred. Soon, he spotted a soldier on a horse standing along the street. Will thought maybe this could be an officer or at least someone more helpful than the pack of soldiers had been. When he asked, the rider said the office was one block to the right, then two blocks along that street, Fort Pitt Road. The rider asked if he was thinking about joining the cavalry, and Will said yes.

"Well then," the officer said, "ask for the 4th Pennsylvania Cavalry. That is my outfit, and I am Major Andrew McCarrier."

Will responded, "My uncle, William A. Eshenbaugh, is a private in your outfit, but I am hoping I can join the 14th Pennsylvania Cavalry, as my father has been a member since the fall of 1862."

Will thanked the major and made his way to the army office. It was a busy place, and there were several men around the front trying to recruit for other outfits, including the infantry, the artillery, and even the navy. Will tied up the black horse and entered the building, one of the biggest and grandest buildings he had seen so far. He saw a short line of men in the corner of the first floor and a poster board that said ARMY on it.

Will joined the line and, after a wait, took his turn at the desk.

"I'm the recruiting sergeant," the man said flatly. "You're here to enlist, are you?"

"Yes, sir," Will answered. "I would like to join the 14th Pennsylvania Cavalry. My father joined the 14th in November 1862, and I want to ride with him."

"Impossible!" barked the sergeant. "New orders from the Secretary of War prohibit fathers and sons or brothers from serving together in the same outfit."

When Will asked why, the sergeant explained that there had been too many families who lost a father and son or multiple brothers at such horrible battles as Gettysburg and Antietam.

"Understood, sir," Will said. "In that case, can I join the 4th Pennsylvania Cavalry? My uncle is with that outfit."

The sergeant confirmed that Will could join the 4th and then asked Will's age and if he could ride a horse.

"I have been riding a horse for many years," Will replied. "In fact, I have my own horse I intend to bring with me."

"Good," the sergeant said. "The army is recruiting men with their own horses and paying for them if the horse and the soldier are in service. I'll need to see the horse to make sure it's acceptable to the army."

Will led him outside to where the black horse stood. Examining the horse, the sergeant said he would personally buy such a fine horse if it were for sale. Will let him know the horse was not for sale, and the sergeant motioned for Will to follow him back inside to finish up his paperwork. He had Will sign his enlistment papers, and they were for a term of three years or the end of the war, stating that his pay would be twelve dollars per month plus two dollars per month for use of the horse. His term would not start until he was mustered in, and that would happen when he got to the training camp in Harrisburg in a few days.

"There's a train leaving tomorrow night," the sergeant said. "It has passenger cars and freight cars attached that will carry the horses and equipment. Take your horse to the end of the wharf tomorrow to get it checked in for transport by the quartermaster."

The sergeant handed Will shipping documents and told him to take the horse to the quartermaster by three p.m. the next day. He also told Will it would be wise to board the car by five p.m. and find a seat about halfway back so he would be away from the cold drafts around the car doors.

10

"I Have Joined the Army"

Will felt elated about being accepted and the prospect of leaving so quickly. He had promised to meet Bossman back at the wharf at noon, but he spotted the post office across the street. Will went in and bought a stamp, a sheet of paper, and an envelope. He borrowed a pencil and wrote a letter.

Mother,

I do not want you to worry. I worked my way to Pittsburgh, and I have joined the army. I will be leaving tomorrow by train to Harrisburg, where I will be sworn into the 4th PA CAV where Uncle William A. serves. They are sometimes close to the 14th where Papa rides.

I have decided this is the right thing for me to do, and I feel a calling to serve.

Your faithful son,

William

Will wrote her name and address on the envelope, added the stamp, and handed it to the postmaster.

He gathered up the black horse and traced his route back to the wharf. With time to spare before his meeting with Bossman, Will strolled along the streets. The city bustled with soldiers, rough-dressed characters, and lots of traders working to fill army orders. Several times, he was asked if the black horse was for sale, and Will would just shake his head and walk on. He realized how hungry he was as he smelled the meats and breads cooking on open fires and being offered to the passing crowds. He finally stopped at one stand and ordered a biscuit, two sausages, and a coffee.

He arrived early at the wharf and saw two wagons being loaded with lumber and the disassembled raft he had ridden on down from Kittanning. In the shade, he saw Bossman resting under a large maple tree. Will joined him, and Bossman said he was pleased with the sale of lumber, as prices were higher now than what they were on his last trip here.

Beside Bossman stood a nice-looking bay gelding horse. Bossman said he had decided to buy a horse since he had a little extra money. With the saddle, tack, and rifle that Will was about to sell him, he could ride back home in style and maybe make it in one day. The Henry .44 repeating rifle would give him good protection against any thieves. Bossman was worried as he carried a lot of money and would not have the protection of any help, what with Will joining the army. They had not seen the other deckhand since they landed.

Will slipped the saddle and saddle pad off the black horse and put both on the bay. The rig fit well, and Will took off the bridle and bit and tried it on as well, with no adjustments needed. Will and Bossman shook hands, and both wished the other well in whatever lay ahead.

⸻ ⧟ ⸻

Will found a bench along the wharf and tied the black horse up beside him as he sat down and took in the scene. His thoughts wandered back to the farm and how Mother must be worrying, but it had felt good to hear that brother Albert had been able to step up to the work.

Will pondered what he should do for the night. He saw the livery stable that might be the one owned by the man they met when the raft landed. Will led the black horse there, tied up, and entered the office. Sure enough, it was the same man.

Will reminded the man that they had spoken down by the dock the previous day at the raft auction of goods. He said he needed a stall for the night for the black horse along with feed. Will added he needed to sleep in the stall tonight as well. The man confirmed that the cost would be fifty cents for the horse and ten cents for the right to sleep in the stall, payable in advance. Will paid and asked if he could have a stall as far from the front door as possible and settled his horse into a stall near the back end of the stable. Will then decided to wander the streets to take in the sights.

⸎

Shortly after dark, Will returned to the stable and checked in on the black horse. All seemed well, and Will cleaned the stall, smoothing out the sawdust on the floor, laid down, and pulled the bearskin coat tight around him. He felt for the big pistol, and it comforted him to feel the grip and know he had it handy if needed.

Will barely had time to pull his coat tight around him before exhaustion claimed him. The stable smelled of warm hay and horse sweat, and the rhythmic sound of the black horse's slow breathing was almost soothing. He drifted off in no time, his body surrendering to the weight of fatigue.

Outside, the night stretched on, silent but for the occasional creak of old wood or the distant hoot of an owl. The black horse dozed on its feet, shifting only slightly in its stall.

Then . . . whispers.

Low. Muted. Sinister.

Will's eyes snapped open. He lay still, listening, his pulse thrumming in his ears. He wasn't alone.

Fingers tightening around the butt of his pistol, he shifted carefully, rolling just enough to get a view of the stable beyond the wooden slats of the stall. A single lantern flickered near the entrance, casting weak, dancing shadows across the walls.

Two men. Moving from stall to stall. Checking horses.

A rustling sound came from the stall next to his. A latch clicked. Hooves shuffled against straw. They were leading a horse out.

Then another latch.

His latch.

A voice hushed but eager. "Now, here's a beauty. Army will pay top dollar for him."

Will's grip tightened on the pistol. The thief hadn't seen him, his coat blending into the shadows against the stall's back wall.

The man reached for the black horse's lead rope.

Will cocked the hammer and fired.

The gunshot shattered the stillness. The bullet punched into the rafters, showering dust and splinters down on the thief's head.

"Hell!" The man stumbled backward, nearly tripping over his own boots.

"Run, dammit!" his partner hissed.

Both men bolted, boots pounding against the wooden floor as they crashed toward the stable door, shoving it open and disappearing into the night.

Will sat up, heart hammering, his pistol still warm in his grip. He listened for a long moment—only the sound of the black horse snorting and shifting restlessly met his ears.

He exhaled slowly, then reached over and latched the stall door tight.

Lying back down, he stared at the ceiling, sleep now a distant thought. His mind turned over the past few weeks—the faces of the outlaws, the thieves, the drunkards.

So many bad men.

And tomorrow, the army.

Would it be any different?

The first light of dawn finally crept through the cracks in the stable walls, and Will let out a breath of relief. At least for now, the night was over.

In the darkness of early morning, Will used the outhouse behind the stable, then stopped at the horse trough to wash his face and hands, wiping them dry on his big coat. The morning seemed warmer than past mornings, so Will decided to hang the coat back in the stall with the black horse and go find a meal.

Up the street stood a large tent set up with rough tables inside and a kitchen in front. Will asked about a meal and was told it would be twenty-five cents for two pancakes, a slice of ham, and a cup of coffee. Will paid and took a seat at the first table, the only person in the tent. As Will waited for his food, another man entered. Obviously injured since he had a sling around his neck supporting his right arm, he also had a walking stick in his left hand to help him navigate. His left leg seemed to be very stiff, and there appeared to be a bandage around his left thigh.

Seeing the man was dressed in buckskin, Will lowered the brim of his hat and did not make eye contact with the stranger. Will's heart raced. Could that be the man he shot, the one he had nicknamed Buckskin? Will snuck another look, finding an uncanny resemblance between this man and the one he shot at the railroad crossing. When his meal arrived, Will quickly gobbled it down, eager to escape the tent as soon as possible.

Will decided his best bet was to lie low all day and then lead the black horse to the wharf later in the day and board the passenger car on the train as early as possible. The more he thought about it, the surer Will became that the man in the tent was indeed Buckskin. And surely that man would recognize the black horse or bearskin coat. At least, this chance encounter assured Will that he had not killed Buckskin but had likely wounded him in both the right shoulder and the left leg.

Back in the stall, the black horse was finishing the grain he had been fed by the stable hand and was about to start on the fork of hay that had been tossed into the stall. Will settled back against the wall and pondered how he would get the horse down to the Union quartermaster without being spotted by Buckskin.

In time, Will wandered around the stable, thinking about his dilemma, when he spotted a half-empty barrel of white-wash with paintbrushes nearby. Will took the barrel and brush to his stall and began disguising the black horse by brushing both back legs from the hoof to the hock. In another couple of minutes, he had a black horse with two white socks. Next, he turned the bearskin coat inside out and gave the lining a few swipes of whitewash as well. He then draped the coat over the back of the black horse.

Returning the barrel and brush, Will waited an hour for the whitewash to dry. He then led the black horse out of the stable and down the street to the quartermaster's desk on the wharf. There, the army clerk asked for Will's paperwork. In a few minutes, the clerk told Will to put the black horse into the paddock next to them. Will pulled the coat off the black horse and led him to the paddock, where he tied the lead rope around the horse's neck and gave the horse a good pat along the neck.

"Sir," Will said, "when can I board?"

"Anytime you want to," the clerk replied. "Just take a seat halfway back in the car. That way, you are away from the doors that do not close well and let a lot of cold air in."

"Much obliged, sir," Will replied with a nod.

Will selected a window seat in the middle of the first passenger car and settled in. He turned the bearskin coat back to right-side out and wrapped himself in its warmth. Soon he was fast asleep and must have slept for over an hour until he heard others entering the car. The boarding continued for a couple of hours. Almost all the men coming on board were young, many appearing too young to be going off to war. A few of them seemed to know one or two other young men, so Will gathered that they must have signed up together. Finally, a young man took the seat beside Will.

"My name's Minteer, Harry Minteer," he volunteered. "From Pittsburgh."

Will introduced himself but said he was from Armstrong County. Harry said he had heard of that county but had never been there.

Minteer said he was twenty years old, had been working as a carpenter's helper, and decided he wanted the adventure of going off to war.

"Being in the cavalry sounds exciting," Minteer added. "Sure must beat being in the infantry and walking every step of the way."

Will asked if he rode a horse much.

"Nope, but I'm looking forward to learning to ride," he answered. "And shoot."

Will thought about Harry's comments and felt glad he already knew how to ride and shoot. He looked around the car and wondered how many others had not learned either of these skills. Will was puzzled to hear languages he did not know and found it curious that others were speaking something other than English.

"Say, have you noticed conversations going on in different languages?" he asked Minteer.

Will's seatmate laughed and asked Will if there were not any Germans, Poles, or Italians in Armstrong County. Minteer said Pittsburgh was full of new arrivals from those countries and from Ireland.

"When they can't find work, the army's twelve dollars a month, plus food and board, don't sound so bad."

The passenger car was crowded, with every seat taken and many men standing. Minteer said he guessed all twenty passenger cars were filled. He also guessed there could be as many as a thousand men onboard the train headed to Harrisburg. Soon, the train whistle screamed, and slowly, with jerks, the train pulled out and started to pick up speed. The clicking of the track and wheels soon had many men nodding off to sleep. Will curled up against the window, ready to rest. As he dozed off, he felt grateful for the advice to board early as some of the late arrivals were left to sleep on the floor in the aisles.

11

You're in the Army Now

Late the next morning, the train came to a halt along a siding. A uniformed soldier entered the car and stood on a front seat and shouted, "Welcome to Camp Harrisburg, your new home for the next two months. You will disembark here and have thirty minutes to use the outhouse, grab a sausage biscuit and a coffee, and assemble in the open field next to the train."

Will had not eaten for a full day, and as stale as the biscuit was, he gobbled it down and gulped his coffee, so strong it made him wince.

The same army man stood on a platform and shouted at the men fresh off the train, telling them to make a line of a hundred men across the field. As the men passed, he counted off for them. He repeated the counting with another line behind them and kept doing this until he had ten lines of a hundred men each. He then shouted that each line is a company, starting with the first line as Company A, the second Company B, and so forth until the last line was called Company J. He then instructed each line to step forward and, on the count of three, to shout out their company letter. He then told each company to count off into groups of ten men each; these would be their squads for training. The first ten men were Squad 1 and so on through Squad 10. He then had each squad shout out their company and squad numbers.

"Now," he instructed, "each company and squad, starting with Company A, Squad 1, will line up at the quartermaster's office to draw your uniforms."

There, they were sent to a large open building and told to take off all their civilian clothes, including underwear, take all personal possessions out of their pockets, and proceed to the next room carrying both their new and old clothes. Once in the new room, they were told to throw the old clothes in a wagon and that the clothes would be burned.

Next, army barbers sheared off the long hair of anyone whose hair length did not meet military regulations. Then the recruits were sent through a cold water dousing to wash off any lice and ticks. Finally, the men were permitted to get dressed in their new army uniforms. Will looked around at the men struggling to put on their uniforms and thought, *What an ill-fitted outfit we are!* Some of the newly enlisted men had pants that were much too long; others had pants that did not reach their ankles.

An army man shouted that if their clothes did not fit, they should trade with someone else. After an hour of clothes swapping, the same soldier shouted for them to get back to the drill field and line up by company and squad. Will and Harry Minteer had initially lined up next to each other, so they ended up in Company C, Squad 1.

⸙

For the next two weeks, every day saw the new soldiers arising before dawn to feed and groom their horses, followed by a quick breakfast of black coffee, biscuits, and beans. Then it was off to the drill field. They learned the ranks from private to four-star general, the military commands for marching orders, and they marched in formations by squad, by company, and then all one thousand together.

Afternoons were spent with the horses. Every session began with the words, "Take care of your horse and your horse will take care of you." Each recruit was taught to curry, brush, and clean the hoofs of their assigned mount. Many of the recruits had never been around a horse, so they had to be taught all the fundamentals.

Next came the orders to saddle up. Each trooper had been issued a McClellan saddle, saddle pad, bridle, scabbard, and saddlebags. The men had been told they were responsible for their equipment and would be charged for anything lost or stolen from them. The sergeant suggested it would be a good idea to initial or mark their equipment and store it in their two-man tent at night.

Will watched in amusement as many of the rookies tried to mount their horses. Some made it on only to find the horse had some buck to it and would throw the rider almost immediately. Apparently, the army was not too careful about the horses they bought and figured a rider would sooner or later conquer mastery of the animal.

Only Will and a few others had brought their horses with them. Those with their own mount were sorted out, and a sergeant took charge of them. He had them run drills, order a trot, lope, or gallop, and run them over logs and across ditches, all to test both the animals and the riders. Will passed all the challenges without difficulty as the black horse was willing to respond, and Will had ridden good mounts all his life.

After a midday pause for biscuits and coffee, the troops were issued their firearms. Under new orders from General Ulysses S. Grant, the cavalry units were being reassigned from strictly scouting to focus on raiding and attacking units. So new firearms were ordered, with each trooper issued a Colt .44 revolver and a Henry .44 repeating carbine. The carbines were designed as a shorter version of the rifle, ideal for mounted troopers to maneuver and fire. Their capacity of fifteen rounds fired by lever action were new to the war, as most rifles in use were single-shot Enfield rifles that required several actions to reload a single shot.

General Grant had been successful on the western battlefields and took Vicksburg, Mississippi, in July of 1863. His grit and willingness to fight made President Lincoln take notice, and he summoned Grant to the White House in late 1863. There, he appointed Grant as the commander of all Union forces with the mandate to take the war to the South and capture their capital, Richmond, Virginia, and bring this war to an end. Lincoln was up for reelection in 1864, and the North was growing tired of the war that was entering its fourth year. Many enlistments made in 1861 and 1862 were for two or three years, and a lot of these were coming to an end in 1864. So the need for recruits was high for the North.

Will felt comfortable with his new firearms and still had his own pistol concealed in his saddlebags. Practice was by squad as the officer in charge explained the function of the pistol and the rifle, how to load them, how to clean them, and how to practice safety for the individual troopers themselves as well as all those around them.

Harry admitted to Will that he had never fired a weapon, having lived in the city, and had never been hunting. Will and Harry shared a two-man tent, so they spent much time talking, with Will explaining how to load, aim, and fire, and what to expect with the kick from the explosion in the chamber.

⸺ ◦∞◦ ⸺

On the firing range, Will proved deadly accurate with both his pistol and carbine. He led his squad in accuracy with his marksmanship, so much so that the officer in charge asked Will if he would consider an assignment to a sniper squad that was being formed up. Will asked him to explain the role of a sniper and recoiled when he was told he would be required to sneak in close to the enemy, conceal himself in a tree or building, and then shoot unsuspecting Rebels when they made themselves visible. Preferably, he would shoot officers. Will was shocked at the concept and felt sick at the very idea of shooting someone who was not engaged in fighting. Will felt greatly relieved when the officer said he understood Will's convictions on the matter and dismissed the idea of him becoming a sniper.

As they entered their second month of training, more and more time was spent on horseback, riding across the surrounding countryside in squads, and sometimes the whole company of nine hundred or so riders went out. Their ranks had been reduced by about one hundred men, as some were badly injured by the horses or with firearms, while others were taken ill with diseases, and at least a dozen or so died from the flu or pneumonia.

The weather had brought cold nights and little snow. Now, near the end of February, the days were warming up. Will was getting anxious to finish this training and get his crossed sabers award acknowledging that he had successfully completed the training. It became increasingly apparent that some of the enlistees would not be approved as troopers, and rumors were that those men would be assigned to the infantry and march to war, not ride into battle.

The March days flew by as springtime started to arrive with sunshine and warm afternoons. Finally, the last day of training arrived. Orders came down to be saddled by six the next morning, with clean and brushed uniform, revolver, and rifle. Recruits would form up by company and squad.

Shortly after daybreak, bugles sounded formation, and officers called their companies to attention. A beautiful black horse ridden by a general appeared from the far end of the grounds and galloped across the field and circled to a group of officers assembled.

The commanding officer barked out congratulations to all the new troopers and introduced them to the general, announcing that they had the special privilege of being addressed by General Philip Sheridan, who had been appointed to command all cavalry forces in the east under General Ulysses S. Grant.

General Sheridan congratulated all the new soldiers and told them they would receive their crossed saber medals from their company officers. He then addressed all five thousand assembled riders.

12

The Campaign to Richmond

"On the orders of President Lincoln and led by General Ulysses S. Grant, I am your commander of all the cavalry here in the east," General Sheridan said. "We are going to Richmond, and we are going to give the Confederates and General Lee a fight like they have not seen so far in this war. You men will no longer just scout and skirmish. You will take the fight to the enemy, and we will send all five thousand under my command into battles. Godspeed, and I hope to get you home safely and soon."

As the troops were led out by company, they made their way back to camp and were ordered to unsaddle, put up their mounts, and return to formation on the field. When assembled, the company commander with his aides pinned the crossed sabers on each trooper's hat. From there, they were assigned to their new company, and Will was given his orders to report to Company A while Harry reported to Company M. Harry had not graded out well on his shooting or riding skills but had shown an outstanding ability to care for his and other horses. He excelled at calming them, caring for wounds, and could shoe any of them.

In late March, the cavalry formed up in columns of four horses abreast and headed south. For the first three days, the ride was pleasant, the days were warm and sunny, and the nights were cool. The soldiers enjoyed plenty of chow every night, and the horses grazed well all night on new spring grass. Word among the enlisted men was that General Grant had his entire army on the move and they were taking a direct route through the Wilderness.

The Wilderness had been prosperous cotton plantations in the 1700s, but cotton depleted the nutrients out of the soil. The growers moved to more fertile land, abandoning their previous fields. Those idle fields slowly reforested but with low-quality, high-density scrub oak and brush. Most military on both sides of the war believed these thousands of acres were too dense and overgrown to move an army through them. General Grant was the exception; through the Wilderness was a straight line south through the Shenandoah Valley to his goal of taking the Confederate capital of Richmond, Virginia. This was supposed to catch the Confederates by surprise, as the predictable route was more to the east to avoid the Wilderness.

During the early morning hours of the fourth day, rain started to fall. Not surprising as spring had come to the Shenandoah Valley and, as all these Pennsylvania troopers knew, the new season brought significant rain with it. Everyone and everything was soaked by the end of the day. The firm soil they had been riding on when dry turned into slippery, clinging mud that caked everything it touched. Worse, the supply wagons and gun caissons sank into the clay, and the teamsters cursed and whipped the teams through mud bogs. In some cases, the heavy rain and clay created so much mud that the wagons sank over the axles. Troops dismounted and pushed wagons that were stuck, often unloading supplies and carrying them ahead so wagons could be freed up and back in use.

Officers ordered the men onward, keeping them on the move till dark and then rousing them in the morning from their cold, miserable sleep well before dawn. The troops continued their relentless surge toward Richmond. Officers shouted encouragement that they were at least halfway through the Wilderness.

One morning, Will was startled awake by what he guessed was a huge thunderstorm. This one was seemingly endless, and the lightning was more glowing red patches than streaks of flashing light in the sky. Bugles blasted everywhere around him, and men scurried about the camp to quickly saddle their horses, check their weapons, load extra ammunition into their saddlebags, and form up.

"Rebel cannon fire!" a trooper shouted, galloping past in a blur of dust and sweat.

The ground trembled beneath Will's horse as the distant thunder of artillery shook the morning air. Orders came down the line—Company A was to mount up and move at a trot.

The first hints of dawn bled across the sky, casting an eerie glow over the battlefield. As the sun rose, Will saw smoke curling across the landscape, thick and black, choking the air with the acrid stench of gunpowder. Union artillery boomed from the east, their shells screaming toward the Confederate lines. The Rebels answered in kind, the earth quaking with each return volley.

Then rifle fire.

Sharp cracks split the air to Will's right. A sudden burst of musketry, close. Too close.

"On the right flank!" someone shouted.

Sergeant Harris didn't hesitate. "Right turn! Draw rifles!"

The order snapped through the ranks like a whip crack. The company wheeled right in a fluid motion, hooves churning up dirt as they pivoted toward the enemy. The moment they faced the source of the gunfire, Harris roared, "Charge!"

Will's heart slammed against his ribs as he leaned forward in the saddle.

The hundred yards between them and the Rebels disappeared in a blur.

Gunfire exploded ahead. The Confederates had taken cover behind a rail fence, dirt and splintered wood flying as they fired their long rifles. They had dug in well, throwing up makeshift earthworks against the rails, but their weapons were slow—after each shot, they had to stand and reload.

Will raised his rifle, fired twice into the smoke. He couldn't tell if he hit anything. There was no time to check. The charge pressed on.

He shoved the rifle into its scabbard, reaching instead for his Colt.

Just as he did, a Rebel stood, taking aim at him over the fence.

Will's breath froze.

But his pistol was already cocked. He fired.

The Rebel jerked backward, arms flailing, before crumpling into the dirt.

Chaos swallowed the battlefield. Union troopers fired into the Confederate line, some wielding drawn sabers, their blades flashing in the smoke-hazed light. The air reeked of sweat, blood, and burnt powder.

The black horse surged forward, nostrils flaring, hooves pounding.

The fence loomed. Will braced.

With a mighty lunge, the horse leaped, clearing the rails in a single bound.

He landed hard between two wide-eyed Rebels.

Both dropped their rifles, hands flying up in surrender.

Others followed, throwing down their arms or turning to flee in a disorganized retreat. The Union riders pressed forward, driving them back, the last shots fading into the smoky dawn.

When the dust settled, the officers counted thirty-five prisoners. Another fifteen Rebels lay still—some dead, some moaning in pain.

A detail was ordered to march the captives to the rear. Will swung down from his saddle, breath coming hard as he took stock of his squad. They were clustered nearby, some grinning in the rush of battle, others staring hollow-eyed at the carnage.

The smell of blood and churned earth filled the air.

The shelling had not stopped.

Explosions rumbled in the distance, cannonballs plowing into the tangled trees, setting fire to the dry underbrush. Soon, the cries of wounded men cut through the morning, their screams rising as flames crept toward them.

No one could reach them.

The heat was too intense.

Will swallowed hard, fists clenching.

No time to dwell.

Company A regrouped with three other companies and was ordered south, scouting for enemy movement. The shelling eased, the cannon fire fading, shifting farther away. Twice, they spotted Confederate cavalry moving along distant ridges, but each time, the enemy slipped away before they could give chase.

The battle was far from over.

But for now, they rode on—toward whatever awaited them next.

⚬⚬⚬

As the day faded, the firing ceased and both sides organized encampments for the night. The army cooks had prepared a meal of beef stew, biscuits, and coffee. Will and his squad were all famished and quickly finished with mess and made sure the horses were tied and watered.

As Will and his squad sat in the dark listening to the sounds of fellow troopers bedding down, they spoke of what they had seen in their first day of war.

They had all been surprised at how much noise had filled the air from the shelling, the firing, and the screaming of dying soldiers and horses.

The sergeant came by, sat for a bit, and smoked his pipe. He said that the company had two of their men killed and eight wounded. Another three were unaccounted for—they could have been taken prisoner, killed but not found, or maybe even deserted. The sergeant said that deserters were the worst kind of scum, as they abandoned others who were depending on them, and that General Grant had ordered deserters to be caught, tried, and shot by a firing squad.

Each company set up picket lines of guards. These were armed soldiers set a hundred yards in front of the campsite. They watched for any enemy movement or any enemy trying to sneak into camp, steal horses, or bayonet sleeping soldiers. The pickets were set to rotate every two hours.

Will drew the first post and took his rifle, pistol, and a long-sheathed knife he had found on the battlefield. His sergeant told him the password for the day was "buttermilk," and he was to stop anyone who came his way and shoot them if they could not give the password. He was shown where to picket and told he would be relieved in two hours. Will settled in with his back to a large oak tree and started staring into the dark for any intruders.

Quiet fell over the valley, and in the far distance wounded men still called out from the places where they had fallen. Both sides sent out corpsmen to retrieve their wounded and dead comrades, an uneasy short truce for the night.

Will heard noises in the dark. His hair seemed to stand on edge along his neckline. Were the rustling sounds in the leaves an enemy trying to sneak up on him or maybe just a racoon scrounging for a meal? The two hours seemed to take all night, but finally he heard someone call his name and whisper, "Buttermilk."

"Who goes there?" was the proper response for Will, and his replacement picket soon settled in. Then Will made his way back to camp and found his squad and bedded down.

Will found it hard to sleep that night. He knew he had been lucky to survive, and he wondered how many comrades from the 4th Cavalry had been lost. How would a mother back home find out her son had been killed? His thoughts drifted to the Rebel he knew he had shot dead away that morning. How old was he, where was he from, how long had he been fighting Yankees, and would his mother ever hear about how he died?

Exhausted, Will finally fell asleep but tossed for the few short hours until the bugle blew for his company to rise and get ready for the next day of battle. After feeding and preparing the black horse, Will grabbed a sausage biscuit and a cup of coffee. Soon, the company commander ordered the men to form up.

That day's orders called for the company to ride hard down the right side of the dug-in Confederate Army and see if they could get south of Lee and his men, cutting them off as General Grant pushed his infantry through the Wilderness. Will followed orders and pulled five days of rations that he'd packed in his saddlebags along with ten quarts of oats for the black horse.

Each day started the same way, with cannon fire opening up right after sunrise and continuing for most of the day. Billowing smoke from the fires, cannons, and muskets made it hard to see the sun or figure what time of day it might be. About a thousand troopers in the 4th Pennsylvania Cavalry along with another four thousand riders—including his father's 14th Pennsylvania Cavalry and the famed Michigan riders under Colonel George A. Custer—all rode hard for the next four days, only occasionally skirmishing with small groups of Confederate riders.

On the fifth morning of this ride, word came down that the best Confederate cavalry led by Colonel J. E. B. Stuart had been spotted, and they seemed to be headed to a critical junction of roads south of Spotsylvania Courthouse. General Sheridan had let it be known that one of his objectives was to take out Stuart and his horsemen. Orders were to shoot any of the boys in gray on sight or take them prisoner if they surrendered. Sheridan rode at the head of his forces, and by noon they had engaged fire with Stuart and his men. Sheridan had vast superiority in numbers, but Stuart held the upper hand in experience and horsemanship with his veterans.

13

Yellow Tavern Fight

When the Union Army had marched north in the summer of 1863, shadowing Robert E. Lee as he headed into Pennsylvania, Major General J. E. B. Stuart and his men had ridden completely around the Union Army, harassing its flanks, capturing any laggards, and confiscating numerous wagons laden with supplies, ammunition, and food. Stuart was perhaps the best of the South's cavalrymen and was a flamboyant leader, who rode with a huge plume feather in his hatband. He led the Cavalry Corps of the Army of Northern Virginia and had been successful in raids against the Union Army as far north as Pennsylvania. General Grant had instructed his Union Cavalry—and specifically General Philip Sheridan—to take General Stuart and the Virginia horsemen out of action.

The road junction critical to both sides was a small settlement known by its landmark, Yellow Tavern. Around noon, the fighting commenced as the main body of Sheridan's Union riders caught Stuart's troops in a deadly crossfire. The superior firepower of the Union repeater fire carbines was too much for the Rebels, who had dismounted and taken defensive positions behind fences and trees next to Yellow Tavern.

A veteran second lieutenant of the Fifth Michigan Cavalry was dismounted and firing his Colt .44 when he turned and saw the unmistakable Stuart, plumed hat and red sash, turn toward the lieutenant. Firing immediately, the Michigan man's bullet struck Stuart, knocking him to the ground, grievously wounded.

Quickly, the Virginia Cavalry horsemen retreated south toward Richmond, taking the body of General Stuart with them. He died the following morning, and General Lee lost his best cavalryman and leader.

The conflict with the Virginia Cavalry had been hotly contested, with combat seen by Will, his uncle William A., and the 4th Pennsylvania Cavalry, as well as his father, Andrew, and the 14th Pennsylvania Cavalry. Colonel Stuart's fatal encounter had effectively brought the fighting to an end.

As the day wore down, the Union cavalrymen rounded up all the stray Rebel forces, some slightly wounded, some on foot on account of their mounts being shot or wounded, and some without any more ammunition to continue fighting. All in all, over four hundred prisoners were taken, with guards detailed to march them north and turn them over to General Grant's forces.

❦

Back at Yellow Tavern, the cavalrymen took a night to celebrate the demise of Confederate General J. E. B. Stuart. Scouts went out to Appomattox Court House and surrounding farms, bringing back several fat hogs, lots of bread, and a good supply of whiskey.

In no time, the hogs were dressed out and fresh pork was roasted over spits, and they feasted along with the bread and fresh eggs purloined from farms that had been feeding the Confederate Army for the past three years. Before long, men were taking mighty swigs of whiskey from the jugs, with laughter and merriment in full swing.

Will checked in with Uncle William A., who had survived the week with no injuries. Will and William A. walked over to the 14th Pennsylvania Cavalry camp area and found Andrew. Hurrying over to embrace his father, Will stopped short when he saw his father had a white bandage around his right hand.

"Nothing to be alarmed about, son," Andrew reassured him. "I was nicked by a Minié ball and will be good as new in a few days."

14

A Boy Has Become a Man

When it was Will's turn to tell of his experiences, he had a hard time describing how he and the black horse had confronted a Rebel, shot and killed him, and then kept right on fighting and even taking prisoners. Will paused and then shared how much it troubled him to have stared down an enemy and taken his life.

For a long while, neither Andrew nor William A. said a word. Finally, his father looked at Will and said, "Son, this war business is tough and hard on an older man like me, so I sure hate to see a young man like you here in the midst of it. Some men who have been in this army for three years have not killed anyone."

Now it was Will's turn to think about a response. Finally, and very softly, he said, "Father, Uncle, this was not the first time I'd shot and killed a man. A man tried to rob Mother and me as he pointed his revolver at her, so I used the big Colt .44 and shot him in the chest and then between the eyes. He would have taken all the money we earned selling our load of potatoes, and he likely would've killed us to keep us from reporting him."

Will went on to relate the rest of the story, how the dead man had a companion who had escaped but had been shot up by Will. He described how Mother was afraid the sheriff would come looking for him. He told of staying with Mrs. McNabb and her children, sharing Christmas with Laura, Sara, and Billy, and providing the tree. He told of his adventures down the river to Pittsburgh and of the shady characters who wanted his black horse and how the Colt .44 sure was handy for chasing off horse thieves.

Andrew leaned back and smoked a bit on his pipe. Finally, he looked at Will and said, "Son, you are only sixteen, but you are a man—a man with a good head on his shoulders and a man with a good heart for knowing what is right and what is wrong. I am proud of you, and I am grateful that you protected Mother and left her with a good amount of money from the potatoes and then sent her wages from your work at the sawmill. Now you need to write to her and let her know you are safe and that you and I are seeing each other as we ride up the Shenandoah Valley to Richmond."

Will was thankful to finally be able to share the horrible story of Blackie and Buckskin and the run that Will had made because of it. Later, he found paper and a pencil and wrote Mother about the evening with Papa and how they were both well. He did not, however, share any of the details of the battle.

❧

The next three days were spent riding hard with General Sheridan toward Richmond, frequently encountering skirmishes with some of the Virginia cavalry. As the troops reached the outskirts of Richmond, they observed that the city was heavily fortified. General Sheridan spent the next day dividing his troops into two groups and sending over two thousand in each direction to ride a circle around Richmond and reconnoiter all gun positions and probe possible points of attack. Later, all the troops met back on the north side of Richmond, and General Sheridan and his staff decided the best course of action was to head back north and report to General Grant.

Will was assigned to ride as an aide to General Sheridan as they rode into General Grant's headquarters camp. Will felt dismayed to hear of General Grant's outrage, and Will knew

General Sheridan was surprised to find Grant angry with him for going off to Richmond even with the news that the cavalry had taken out General Stuart. Grant said he had really needed Sheridan's support for the finish of the Wilderness campaign. Grant allowed as how his losses had been high, but he was closer to Richmond than any Union general had been after three years of war.

Grant then softened a bit and shared a story with General Sheridan, referred to as "Little Phil" but addressed by General Grant as Phil. He told of marching troops southeast on a road in the Wilderness after a severe two days of losses. He said he heard from several veterans that they expected when they marched to the crossroads that they would turn north and find a place to rest for a month or two, resupply, and try to figure out General Lee's plans.

Much to the veterans' surprise, when they got to the crossroads, General Grant was sitting on his horse, his uniform muddy, but he used his saber to point the marchers south toward Richmond. The troops cheered the new leader and his desire to fight. Grant said he was so pleased after the criticism of his decision to fight through the Wilderness to be cheered by his veterans for his decision.

⸺ ∞ ⸺

After the ride back from Richmond, the 4th Pennsylvania Cavalry was given a rest period. Horses were tired, men were exhausted, and it was time for Will to give the black horse a complete check-over. He appeared to have lost a little weight from the hard ride and had a few nicks and scrapes on his legs from the rough country. Will led him over the next morning to Company M and found Harry Minteer hard at work shoeing a trooper's horse. Will was glad to see Harry, and as soon as he was finished with the shoeing, he took a seat and asked Will to join him for a cup of coffee. After pouring coffee for both, Harry pulled up a couple of nail kegs for seats.

Harry said he'd been working night and day to patch up horses that had been wounded and replacing worn or lost shoes on every horse that came to him. He wanted to hear all the details of Will's first month in combat. Harry said he had seen both William A. and Andrew in the past day or two, and they had survived without a scratch, although Andrew showed Harry where a bullet had passed through his hat and where one had creased the rump of his horse.

"Will," Harry said, "I'm afraid I have bad news from the Wilderness fight. Bill McNabb was hit hard on his left arm and evacuated to a hospital in Washington, D.C. I received a letter from my family in Kittanning who heard from Mrs. McNabb, and I know you were close to her and stayed there for a while before joining the army."

Both sat silently engaged in thoughts of this bad news. The Union Army had taken control of the railroads north of Spotsylvania Courthouse and had developed an efficient system of bringing supplies south from Washington and Philadelphia and evacuating wounded troops back north to hospitals in those two cities. Will thought of the three little McNabb children and how happy they had been with the small pine tree for Christmas. He felt a little guilty that he had left their house with them asleep and had not taken time to say good-bye. He told Harry he would keep Mr. McNabb and the family in his prayers.

Will left the black horse with Harry to be reshod and walked over to the encampment of the 14th Pennsylvania Cavalry. They, too, were given time to rest and refresh the troops, horses, and equipment. He was glad when he found his father, and they sat and talked more about the fighting they had both seen since the start of the Wilderness campaign. Andrew said he could not remember any tougher terrain or fighting conditions in his time in the war.

He and Andrew talked about the fight against J. E. B. Stuart and the Virginia Cavalry at Yellow Tavern and how glorious it felt to be there when one of Colonel Custer's troopers mortally wounded Stuart. As they discussed the fierce combat of that day, a strange-looking wagon and team rolled by. It had a canvas covering and a driver wearing civilian clothes and a top hat.

Andrew saw Will's look of wonderment and shared that this was the famous photographer Matthew Brady, who was making photographs of battle scenes and soldiers at war and selling them to newspapers. He said Brady was also doing photographs of soldiers and maybe he and Will could get one done of the two of them to share back home. Will had never seen a photograph, let alone been in one, so he was excited and promised Andrew that he would be honored to have a photograph together.

Turning to other matters, Andrew asked if he had any word from home. Will said he had not heard from Mother, but he had just heard from Harry Minteer that Bill McNabb had been wounded at the dawn charge up a hill against dug-in Confederates just north of Spotsylvania Courthouse. Mr. McNabb had been evacuated to a hospital in Washington by rail.

Will shared with Andrew how much he had enjoyed the hospitality of the McNabb household before floating down the Allegheny River to Pittsburgh. As he did with Minteer, he shared with Andrew of his affection for the three McNabb children and the story of dragging the small pine tree in for Christmas and stringing popcorn garlands.

For the next two weeks, Will and the cavalry troops repaired any equipment damaged in the hard campaign and went to the quartermaster for replacements of any lost or unusable equipment. Much to the surprise of the troopers, the government entered charges of what was owed by any trooper who lost or damaged equipment. They were told the charges would be deducted from their pay.

15

Back at the Farm

Mother washed her hands, wiped her face, and took a seat at the kitchen table. She lit a kerosene lantern and gazed out the window from the kitchen. It was mid-June, her favorite time of the year when the days were longer and the smell of fresh grass, new flowers, and trees blossoming made the air smell so beautifully.

She'd had a long day. Albert planted his first crop of potatoes, and she showed him how to mark the spacing for the next row so he could later cultivate between the rows. After spending a couple of hours with Albert early in the morning in the potato patch, Mother harnessed and hitched one of the young horses to the buggy and tied it in front the house. She and the girls freshened up with clean dresses and aprons. Mother loaded all the children in the rear of the buggy and on the seat beside her. She clucked softly, and the horse began moving down the driveway and up the hill toward West Sunbury, about a mile away.

As Mother drove along, she looked over the fields on the farm. The new corn had sprouted nicely even though it was a late crop, the spring rainy season having lasted so long. As they dropped down the hill into West Sunbury, she noticed that the streets were empty, even though it was Saturday morning. Most of the men were, of course, off to the war, so there was much less commerce and far fewer farm wagons in the street.

She pulled up in front of the post office, across the street from the Kohlmeyer grocery store and tied the horse to the hitching rail. She told the children to stay in the buggy. She always marveled at the unique smell of the post office, which was a combination of old lumber, oiled floors, and the winter fire that burned in the iron stove in the lobby.

Mr. Haydon, the postmaster, always looked the same with a string tie, suspenders, and green eyeshade.

"Good morning," he said cheerfully. "It's good to see you."

"Same to you, Mr. Haydon," she replied. "Would you happen to have any mail for me in general delivery?"

"As a matter of fact, I have two letters for you. Let me get them."

She had been expecting one from either her husband or her son, and she wondered if anyone else had written to her. The army had a policy of free postage for servicemen who wanted to write home, so she was hearing from Andrew and Will more often than she thought she might.

The postmaster returned and handed her the two letters. She glanced at the first envelope, and sure enough, it had Will's name and his outfit written up in the left-hand corner. The other one surprised her a bit as it was from Laura McNabb in Kittanning. She slipped both envelopes into her apron pocket, thanked Mr. Haydon, and bid him a good day. Back outside, she told the girls to unload from the carriage and cross the street to the Kohlmeyer grocery store.

It was a general store that sat at the crossroads of five different highways or roads, so the store was usually busy. The children were delighted to see all the merchandise on display. Mother thought the shelves looked light on inventory and figured it was because of the war. She didn't buy much in stores as almost everything she needed was homemade or home-grown: clothes, food, baked bread, and churned butter. But today she had a short list of sugar, salt, flour, thread, needles, and a bolt of cloth to make dresses for the girls. She was able to find everything she needed quickly, and, of course, the children were eyeing the penny candies.

At that, Mr. Kohlmeyer looked at Mother and winked. "I have a special today," he whispered. "It'll be two pieces of candy for the price of one."

So, for a nickel and a penny, Mother was able to get twelve pieces of candy to share two each with Annis, James, Samuel, Alberta, and Priscilla, and a piece to take home for Albert and one for herself.

Back home, Mother decided to do the laundry, since it was a dry and sunny day. She heated the washtub and, along with the girls, churned all the dirty clothes and then wrung them out. They carried the wet laundry to the clothesline, where they hung them out to dry, knowing they probably wouldn't be dry until sometime later the next day.

As a rule, they didn't do any extra work other than chores on Sundays, believing the Bible's principle of observing the Sabbath rest, but Mother decided she would have to take the laundry in on Sunday. To ease her conscience, she made the decision to get her family all up early the next day and go to church.

Because so many men were away, not many families attended church. In fact, the pastor who had led the local congregation for many years, Reverend Isaac Decker, had resigned and led a contingent of young men away to the war as well. He served as a chaplain somewhere in Virginia. In his place, the church had a young preacher, who made the circuit throughout the region, preaching sporadically at various small churches and guiding the church members as best he could.

That evening, Albert gave a report on having completed the planting of his potatoes, and Mother said she was so proud of him. He had learned so well from watching and helping Will and his father before the war. Albert said he was dead tired and going to bed early. Mother helped dispatch the younger children off to bed after giving them a bath, as was tradition on Saturday evening. Finally alone in front of a lantern at the table, she pulled out her two new letters.

She opened the one from Will first. He told her of camp life, how pretty the mountains in the Shenandoah Valley were on the other side of the valley, and that they had been resting for a couple of weeks after several grueling days of engagement with the enemy.

Dear Mother,

We finished a long ride all the way to Richmond and back to Spotsylvania Courthouse. The cavalry was able to finally beat the Virginia Cavalry that for so long had been trouble to all the boys in blue.

I want to share that I have been able to see Father and Uncle William A. almost daily. They are fine and healthy, and we are anxious to bring this terrible war to an end and be home soon.

While we are all doing well, several men have been sick from swamp fever or "the scooches," an odd description for what the doctors call malaria and dysentery. Either illness is disabling and even deadly. Father shared that in his experience of almost three years in the army, almost as many men die from diseases as from battle. He told me to be very careful not to drink any water on the battlefield, as the streams are contaminated from the death and destruction.

Mother, I miss being at home so very much. I hope that Albert is getting the potatoes planted, and I hope Annis, Alberta, and Priscilla are growing into helpful hands around the house and garden. I trust James and Samuel are learning to tend to farm chores.

We all hope to be home by summer, and I send my love to you and the family.

Love from your son,
William

16

A Letter from Laura

Mother had tears in her eyes and dropped her head, saying a prayer for both Will and Andrew, for their safe and soon return from the war.

After she wiped her tears away, she used her paring knife to slit open the letter from Laura McNabb. Mother was quite concerned about what the contents might be. She thought about Laura and their friendship over the years. Mother's family, the Dixons, were good friends with the McNabb family and in turn good friends with the Minteers.

Mother had not seen Laura since before the war, but she had heard from her and knew that in addition to her daughter Laura Ann, she also had given birth to daughter Sara Ada and son Billy. She remembered how concerned Laura had been when her husband, William, had enlisted in August 1861 for a three-year hitch. He had safely endured many battles and was now within two months of his enlistment's end.

Laura's letter came right to the point.

My dear Mary Ann,

My beloved Will was injured in battle in early May and had been removed from the battlefield at Spotsylvania Courthouse by train to the hospital in Washington, D.C. I just received a letter from the Department of Army that William died on June 8 from his wounds. He was buried in a new national cemetery for soldiers across the river from Washington.

I had been worried sick about William's injuries, and his only letter home was written from the hospital by a nurse. He convinced me that he was recovering and would be home soon.

I am devastated at his loss, and I despair what I'm going to do with three youngsters at home with no income.

The army had indicated that I will get a short-term settlement of five dollars a month, which would be far less than the twelve dollars per month William had been earning. I now have so much regret that I did not go to Washington, D.C., to see William, and now he is buried hundreds of miles from home.

I will keep you apprised of my plans and how we are going to cope with the loss of my husband.

Love and Godspeed to you and your men who are still in harm's way,
Laura McNabb

Mother broke into tears and sobs. The strain and emotion of the war—with Andrew and Will off fighting, the daily hardship of keeping the farm going, and now William's death—seemed more than she could bear. She found herself on an uncontrollable sobbing spell as she felt overwhelmed with the burden of raising the family, tending the farm, and wondering what would happen to her if Andrew did not come home from the war. She had her head down on the table and was startled when someone's hand touched her shoulder. Albert had heard her sobbing and came downstairs to console her. She wiped her eyes, regained composure, and shared with Albert the loss of William McNabb.

Mother had a restless night thinking of the grief Laura McNabb must be suffering and how bleak the future must seem to her. She arose early and roused the children with the announcement that they were going to church this morning. Before the war, Andrew insisted they all attend every Sunday, and he would harness the horse and hitch up the buggy in good weather or the sleigh in the wintertime. Then off they would go for the ride into town. This morning, Mother was quiet during the ride and had handed Albert the reins. She was deep in thought.

There was a very small gathering at the church, despite the beautiful weather. During the announcements, the young preacher said several Butler County men had been captured during the battles in the Wilderness and were being shipped by the Confederates to a new prisoner-of-war camp in southern Georgia near Andersonville. He said the new position of General Grant was to no longer exchange prisoners of war, so the pastor urged everyone to pray for all the men sent to Andersonville. As he got more information about the list of prisoners, he would share it at a future service.

Mother rose to ask the congregation to keep the family of William McNabb in their prayers, sharing that William had succumbed to his wounds less than two months before his three-year enlistment would have been up. She mentioned the irony that William had survived the terrible combat at Antietam in the fall of 1862 and the three days of heavy fighting at Gettysburg in July 1863.

As the family rode home from church, Mother fell quiet again as she thought about what Mrs. McNabb must be going through. Mother decided she would write a letter that afternoon. She was going to invite Mrs. McNabb and her three children to come live on the farm if things were too tough to maintain in Kittanning. She could use the company, and Mrs. McNabb might financially need to give up the house and have a place to go.

17

Combat Ready

On a beautiful summer afternoon in Virginia, Will found time to take a dip in the river and wash his clothes. His sergeant had put his squad on alert that orders could come down Sunday night or Monday, meaning they would soon get back in the saddle and back into combat.

Will curried and brushed out the black horse and used light oil on his saddle and saddlebags to have them ready for whatever would come next. He also found time to sit down and write a letter to Mother back in Pennsylvania. He shared with her how much he had enjoyed visiting with his father and Uncle William A. He told her it was likely they would be back in the saddle in the next few days, but no one had any idea where they would be going or what they would be doing. He said he prayed every night that the war would end soon and that he, Father, and Uncle William A. would make it home together.

Will lay on his ground cloth in the pup tent. These early June evenings were comfortable, but he couldn't sleep. The sergeant had gathered the men around and told them that they needed to be up by three a.m. and would be on a hard ride for the next three or four days.

"Men," he said, "for many of you this will be the first time you'll have to shoot someone, and it may be up close. I know it's hard and against everything you were taught when you were raised as a child. But if you don't shoot the enemy, he is going to shoot you. I don't want to have to write a letter to your mother tomorrow night or later this week. If the other man is wearing gray, shoot him. And as soon as you shoot one, be looking for the next one. There will be thousands of us there, and there will be thousands of them shooting back at you."

The sergeant went on to tell his troops that if they had the chance to capture a regiment flag from the Confederates, they should bring it back and enjoy a hero's celebration. Doing so would likely mean shooting a young boy, because the flags were normally carried into battle by someone who couldn't fight.

"Don't hesitate, because that flag is what tells the enemy where to be," the sergeant said. "I'll give the orders, but it's likely that our first round of fire will be from horseback using your carbine. As we get closer, it'll be time to put the Henry in the scabbard and pull your pistol. Look for me and look for a company flag if you lose position. If you hear retreat, do exactly that. We will regroup, but we may have found ourselves outnumbered in a particular location. If your horse goes down, try to grab your carbine and shoot from behind your horse, or grab a loose horse and remount. If you get into close quarters or run out of pistol ammunition, draw your saber and use it to slash any Confederate around you."

He explained that the mission would be to secure the railroad and highway crossing that was currently lightly guarded by the Confederate cavalry.

In midsummer of 1864, General Sheridan was given command of 39,000 troops, comprised of 15,000 cavalry riders and 24,000 infantrymen. Within that large collection of troops were three companies—the Fifth, Seventh, and Nineth Michigan Cavalries—under the command of Brigadier General George Armstrong Custer.

Custer graduated third from the bottom of his class at West Point but had risen to distinction during the Civil War to be a daring cavalry officer, unafraid to lead a charge into enemy lines.

The Shenandoah Valley throughout the war had been a haven for the Confederate Army. It was occupied by many pacifist immigrants and farmers from European descent, primarily the Dunkers and the Amish. They refused to fight for either side, content to grow their crops and sell them to the highest bidder. Because they were the breadbasket of the Confederate Army, General Grant instructed General Sheridan to scorch the earth as he progressed up the Shenandoah Valley. By that, he meant Sheridan's men should round up all livestock, take any food and clothing they could carry, and burn the barns and equipment. They should leave nothing in the way of resources behind that would help the Confederate Army. This eventually earned Sheridan's troops the name "Pennsylvania Barn Burners."

General Robert E. Lee was trying to lead his army south of the city of St. Petersburg, Virginia. He had seen success against a larger Union Army under General Grant at Cold Harbor. That had been a decisive victory for the Confederates and came at the cost of twenty thousand Union soldiers killed or wounded. The Union Army had been slow to arrive at Cold Harbor, and General Lee's men constructed a front almost seven miles long.

The cavalry had withdrawn to the hillside above the battlefield. Will and his mounted companions watched in horror as one wave after another of Union infantrymen charged the Confederate position, only to be mowed down as they crossed the open areas in front of the fortification. Will's ears rang from the sound of cannon fire from the Confederates on top of the hillside. Men lay dying, suffering from their mortal wounds and crying out for help and water. Unfortunately, they were in a no-man's land between the two armies as a battle raged all around. There was nothing the cavalry could do to help them.

The horse soldiers' role was to support the ends of the lines and look for an opportunity to charge the flanks of the Confederates, but no such opening occurred.

As Will watched the infantrymen, it appeared to be an extremely confused and chaotic scene to him. Riders charged back and forth across the Union ranks. Infantrymen arrived late to the battlefield, some not ready to fight until four o'clock in the afternoon in a battle that had started at dawn. As darkness fell, both sides broke off fighting but stayed in place. Will's company bedded down for the night without any fires and went to bed with cold biscuits for supper.

At four a.m., the Confederate cannons commenced to fire again from the bluffs. At dawn, Will and the other cavalrymen could see Union Army infantrymen showing up again for the day, mounting new charges against the Confederates. Today's battlefield saw a repeat of yesterday's battle, with thousands of troops in blue uniforms rushing toward the dug-in Confederates at the top of the hill only to be mowed down, often falling on top of comrades who had been mowed down the previous day. Around one p.m., a retreat was sounded by the Union forces, and the troops withdrew from the battlefield.

Early the next morning, General Sheridan had his troops on the march headed to the southwest. Their destination was a railroad crossing and warehouses at Trevilian Station. General Lee was concerned that this was a plan to try to lead General Grant's army around Lee and head south toward Richmond. So General Lee sent two cavalry divisions to meet the three divisions under General Sheridan. Both sides rode hard for two days to reach this critical rail station.

With General Sheridan's troopers ready, they met the Confederates head-on. Just as the sergeant had instructed, Will and his company went in with their carbines blazing. This was a decisive advantage for the north. They were equipped with new

Henry .44 caliber repeating rifles, an innovation that held fifteen rounds of ammunition. Will had learned that if the enemy rider did not provide a good target, he should shoot the horse as a cavalryman on foot was not a great fighting force.

Right after chow on Sunday evening, the bugle sounded for assembly, and the troops all fell in on their parade field. Orders came down that they were to be ready to mount up by six a.m. Monday morning, taking five days of rations for themselves and five days of grain for their horse. They were also told to pack 120 rounds of ammunition and to bring their carbines and pistols as well as their sabers for the ride. With that, the assembly was dismissed and the men returned to their quarters.

The bugle blew at 4:30 a.m., rousting out the troopers. They quickly fed their mounts, led them to the watering hole, and then tied them off. Then the men grabbed their breakfast, picked up their rations and grain from the quartermaster, and filled their saddlebags. With the troops gathered on the assembly field at 6:00 a.m., General Sheridan rode up in the breaking dawn on his big black stallion, and the men were called to attention.

"Gentlemen," the general called out, "we shall ride out on the double-quick trot, headed south to assist General Grant. It is our intention to take the capital of Richmond from the Confederates and hopefully force their surrender. We believe General Lee is in a weakened condition, that his men are running short of food for themselves, feed for their livestock, and ammunition for their weapons. We will capture all livestock in our path and bring it back to our quartermaster. We shall destroy any crops that we cannot carry off and burn every barn of anyone who has supported the Confederacy for the last three years as we march south. It is time that the Shenandoah Valley stopped being the breadbasket for the Confederate Army. We will turn it to our advantage, and we will turn it to their disadvantage. We shall ride hard, we shall fight hard, and we shall not retreat."

18

At Trevilian Station

Both Union cavalry from the north and the Confederates from the south rode hard to be the first to reach Trevilian Station and the vital railroad junction there. Will figured there were about fifteen thousand Union troops, and others had heard that some ten thousand Confederate cavalrymen remained. The Rebels were without their famed cavalry officer J. E. B. Stewart, and the Union was led by a fearsome fighter in General Sheridan, accompanied by the redoubtable Brigadier General George A. Custer.

Will had never seen so many horses, nor had anyone else seen this many mounted riders throughout the whole Civil War. History would record later that this was the largest fight in the entire war fought entirely by cavalry units.

Will's company had meant to outflank the Rebels, but the plan fell apart as fast as the smoke thickened. Gunfire cracked like whips in every direction, and in a blink, the maneuver dissolved into bloody chaos. Men screamed. Horses reared. The air was a storm of lead and steel.

Will barely had time to fire more than a couple of rounds from his Henry before the enemy was on them. He dropped the rifle to his side and yanked the Colt .44 from his hip.

"Come on then!" he growled through clenched teeth.

Six shots rang out in rapid fire. The first two dropped a pair of Rebels straight from their saddles. Another staggered backward, clutching his chest, before crumpling. Will didn't stop to watch them fall, quickly reloading his pistol.

He looped the leather lanyard around his wrist with practiced speed, the gunmetal cold and familiar in his grip. The black horse danced beneath him, nostrils flaring, muscles rippling with barely contained fire.

"Easy, boy! Hold steady!"

But the horse relished the excitement. He spun and lunged, hooves flashing dangerously near enemy troopers. Will emptied the revolver in a blur, cutting down two more Rebels—one blown from his saddle, another pitching forward with a scream. He didn't pause, again reloading with precision.

"One more," he muttered, "then it's steel and grit."

His breath came short now, his shoulder throbbing from recoil, the heat unbearable. The Colt bucked in his hand again and again. A Rebel officer yelled something guttural and charged—but Will was faster. One shot. Center mass. The gray-clad soldier flipped from his horse like a rag doll.

Then pain. White-hot. A slash across his right thigh like fire under his skin.

"Damn!" Will wheeled the black horse right and caught the gleam of a saber. A Rebel trooper on the ground, eyes wide with hatred, swung again. Will didn't think—he fired point-blank. The man folded to the earth, saber clattering beside him.

Click. Click.

The pistol was empty.

"Hell."

Letting the Colt hang limp from his wrist, Will drew his saber, the steel hissing from its sheath. A Rebel officer streaked by on horseback—Will swung hard but missed. Before he could circle around, a Union bullet caught the officer square in the chest. The man toppled, lifeless, right in front of Will's horse.

Will didn't wait for the next threat. Blood soaked his pants, the leg numb and burning all at once. He turned the black horse toward the edge of the fray.

"We're done here, boy."

They galloped out of the melee and into the tree line. Safe—for now. Will reined in under the sparse cover and slid his saber away. Then he looked down.

His leg was torn open—an ugly, red gash, nearly a foot long, pouring blood.

"Damn that saber . . ."

He pulled his belt free and looped it above the wound. Every tug to tighten it felt like lightning in his spine, but he gritted his teeth and yanked hard until the bleeding slowed.

"Gotta move," he whispered, patting the horse's neck. "We're not dead yet."

Every jolt from the saddle was agony, but Will forced himself to stay upright. They made their way past the battlefield, toward the rear lines where the Union medics and supply wagons were stationed.

By the time they reached the train station, the place was swarming with moaning men, bloodied limbs, and the stench of death. Will's stomach twisted. Bodies everywhere. Some alive, some not. A surgeon barked orders. Orderlies ran with stretchers. Cries of "Over here!" and "Hold him down!" cut through the air.

Will turned the black horse away. He wasn't ready to lie in the dirt waiting for a surgeon's knife.

Instead, he rode wide, behind the wagons, until he saw the blacksmith shop.

There was Minteer—his old friend—sleeves rolled, tending to a horse with a bloodied flank. Will nudged the black horse forward. Minteer looked up and froze.

"Will!" he shouted. "Good God, your leg!"

Will tried to dismount but nearly collapsed, the pain searing.

"Stay put!" Minteer ran to him. "Don't move. Just hand me your pistols and rifle."

Will, breathing hard, did as told.

"Guess I ran out of bullets," he said with a tired grin.

Minteer took the rifle, gave Will a once-over, and muttered, "Looks like you almost ran out of blood too."

Will's voice was low and raspy as he described the horror unfolding inside the station. "The whole damn place looks like a slaughterhouse," he said. "They're stacked in lines—some missing arms, some legs. Blood everywhere. And the screaming . . ." He trailed off, shaking his head.

Harry frowned deeply, gently taking the reins of the black horse. "Come on, let's get you seen," he said, leading them around the far side of the station, away from the chaos. The black steed snorted and resisted at first, ears pinned, still wired from the adrenaline of battle, but Harry kept a firm hand.

He tied the black horse to a hitching post and disappeared through the side door of the station. Minutes later, he returned with two orderlies—young, grim-faced, and spattered with dried blood. They were Harry's pals, and from the way they moved, they knew time was precious.

"We got a spot," one of them said, nodding toward the rear. "Private. Superintendent's office. Desk's clear."

Will managed a weak smirk. "Glad to bleed all over executive furniture."

The orderlies chuckled and then gently lifted him onto the stretcher. Will clenched his jaw as pain flared through his thigh like lightning. The moment they entered the building, the heat and stench hit him like a brick wall—sweat, blood, bile, and something else, something rotting.

He turned his head and instantly wished he hadn't. A pile of severed limbs—arms, legs, even a child-sized foot—lay heaped like firewood in the corner. An orderly with a wheelbarrow was shoveling them like trash, grumbling to himself as he wheeled the grotesque cargo out over the freight dock.

Will gagged. "Lord, have mercy."

One of the orderlies carrying him said softly, "Don't look, soldier. Just hold on."

They passed through a narrow hallway and into the superintendent's office. The wooden desk had been cleared off and hastily covered with a clean army blanket. The orderlies lifted Will carefully and laid him across it. He gripped the edges, knuckles white.

Moments later, a surgeon swept in, his white apron soaked red from earlier procedures. He was a stocky man, mid-fifties, sleeves rolled and eyes sharp with battlefield efficiency. His tool bag hit the floor with a heavy thud.

"Cut the pant leg and drawers above the wound," he barked.

The orderlies obeyed quickly, slicing away the fabric. When they pulled off Will's boot, dark blood spilled out, pooling on the floorboards beneath the desk.

The surgeon peered down at the injury and nodded. "Lucky son of a gun," he said.

Will arched an eyebrow, barely able to speak. "Don't feel lucky."

"Cut's deep but runs along the muscle. No bone damage I can see. You'd be screaming a lot more if it was. Saber strike, not a bullet. That's good. No lead fragments to dig out."

He reached into the wound with his fingers, probing for damage. Will let out a raw scream, arching off the desk, sweat pouring from his face.

"Hold him!" the surgeon snapped.

One of the orderlies pressed down on Will's shoulders while the other gripped his hand.

"Bite this." The surgeon handed him a thick wooden stick. Will took it between his teeth just as the doctor began cleaning the wound with a harsh, burning chemical that felt like fire in an open nerve.

Will groaned deep in his throat, biting down so hard the wood creaked.

"You're doing fine," the doctor said, more to his tools than to Will. "Let's get this stitched before he passes out."

One stitch. Two. Five. Ten. Each one sent waves of agony crashing through Will's body. He couldn't breathe, couldn't think—only endure. The edges of his vision went black.

Finally, the surgeon leaned over him, his voice a muffled echo.

"All done. Bandaged and wrapped. Keep that dressing on for two weeks. If you're still breathing by then, you'll probably dodge the fever. Try walking after that—keep the leg from locking up."

Will nodded weakly, too spent to speak.

The surgeon motioned to the orderlies. "Get him out of here. Next!"

Outside, the air was marginally fresher, though still heavy with the smoke of battle and burned powder. They laid him on the grass in front of the station, and Harry appeared by his side again, his face drawn with worry.

"Bring him to the blacksmith shop," Harry ordered. "I'll watch over him myself."

The orderlies obeyed without question.

Beside the train station stood a massive warehouse, its double doors flung open to reveal Confederate supplies—barrels of grain, crates of rifles, bolts of cloth, and several towering bales of cotton.

"Take what we can use," an officer shouted to passing troopers. "The rest we'll burn."

Union soldiers moved quickly, loading wagons with the most valuable goods. Meanwhile, others unrolled cotton across the station floors and lawn, creating makeshift beds for the wounded. Each man who emerged from surgery was given a clean mat to lie on—something soft, at least, after so much pain.

Down by the railroad tracks, soldiers stacked the remaining cotton bales into a towering pyramid. Then one of them struck a match.

The fire roared to life with a whoosh, flames leaping into the twilight sky. The Confederate supplies meant for a lost cause were now smoke and ash.

Lying near the blacksmith's forge, Will watched the fire rise, the orange glow dancing across his pale, sweat-soaked face. Harry knelt beside him, wiping his brow with a wet cloth.

"You hang in there," he said softly. "You'll ride again. This horse isn't done with you yet."

Will's lips twitched into a faint smile. "Neither am I."

⸙

For the next two days, the valley echoed with the clang of hammers, the groan of straining mules, and the crackle of roaring flames. Union troopers, grim faced and relentless, tore up mile after mile of Confederate railroad track. Iron rails screamed as they were pried from their wooden beds, then stacked like cordwood beside piles of timber ties.

"Fire it up!" a sergeant shouted, and a group of soldiers tossed kerosene onto the stacked ties. A match was struck, and with a loud *whoosh*, flames leapt skyward.

As the fire reached a blistering heat, teams of men heaved the iron rails onto the inferno. The steel turned from black to orange to a furious red.

"Now!" came another shout. Mules were hitched to both ends of the glowing rails. Grunting, sweating soldiers guided them around nearby trees, forcing the hot iron to bend like taffy. With loud groans and screeches, the rails curled into U shapes—twisted beyond repair.

Will watched from his resting spot near the blacksmith's forge, his leg bound tight in fresh bandages. He squinted at the red-hot rails and muttered, "Looks like a blacksmith's worst nightmare."

Harry sat nearby, sharpening his saber with slow, methodical strokes. He glanced over. "They call it a Pennsylvania bow tie," he said. "Sherman used them in Georgia. Railroads don't run when you got no straight rails."

Will smirked faintly. "That's one way to stop the supply lines."

For miles in both directions from the station, rails lay bent like snapped bones. Smoke rose across the countryside, not just from the rails but from barns, storage sheds, and any depot the Rebels might have used. It was the slow, grinding destruction of an army's backbone—and every man knew it.

Inside the warehouse, the transformation was heartbreaking. What once held Confederate supplies now brimmed with rows of wounded soldiers. Cots and cotton mats lined every inch of floor space, and the stench of antiseptic barely masked the odor of blood and sweat.

Nurses—many volunteers who had followed the army— arrived with quiet resolve. Dressed in simple uniforms, they moved through the sea of injured with gentle hands and steady hearts.

"Easy now, soldier," one whispered, dabbing sweat from a boy no older than sixteen. His leg was gone from the knee down. He didn't cry—just stared at the rafters in shock.

The groans never stopped. Some screamed in their sleep; others begged for water or mercy. Many called out for their mother. And each dawn, the sun rose over a new round of death.

Soldiers wrapped in blankets were carried out in silence, their faces hidden. A grim procession.

Union ambulance wagons rolled up every hour, their wheels caked with mud and blood. The dead were carted away without ceremony. The living—those strong enough to endure the ride—were loaded into other wagons bound for a rail junction twenty miles north.

There, they would be transferred to hospital trains—wooden cars converted to clinics on wheels—bound for Washington or Philadelphia. If they made it that far, they might live.

By the end of the week, General Sheridan's orders arrived. It was time for the cavalry to regroup. The valley mission was done, and every man capable of holding a rifle was needed at the front.

The camp buzzed with movement. Wagons were loaded, horses saddled. The ring of iron on iron echoed once more as blacksmiths packed up their tools.

Minteer found Will where he lay near the forge, propped on a bed of straw.

"You're riding with us," Minteer said gruffly, but his eyes were kind. "Farrier's wagon has a soft spot between the barrels. It won't be smooth, but it won't kill you either."

Will nodded, wincing as he tried to shift his leg. "Sounds like I'll be riding in style."

Harry led the black horse over, reins in hand. The stallion had been curiously calm around Will since the injury—almost protective.

"I'll tie him to the back of the wagon," Harry said. "He'll follow you home, like he always does."

Will reached out, brushing a hand along the horse's neck. "Don't let him wander. He's the only thing I got that doesn't leak blood."

Harry chuckled and helped Will into the wagon, settling him onto a folded canvas tarp cushioned by blankets. Will grimaced but didn't complain.

As the cavalry pulled out, the black smoke of the destroyed railroad still curled into the sky behind them. The ruined station, the amputated limbs, the cries of the wounded—they all faded into the distance.

Will lay on his back, the wagon jolting beneath him, his saber resting beside him and the black horse's steady hoofbeats keeping time like a drum.

They were heading north, toward the next fight. Toward whatever came next.

And Will was still alive.

19

Mail Call

Saturday evening chow was usually followed by mail call by the sergeant. Most men looked forward to it. The mail service had become more efficient with the Union control of the rail lines from Washington D.C., Philadelphia, and Harrisburg, Pennsylvania, to the central part of Virginia.

With Will still on crutches, he and Harry slowly made their way so that they could hear the sergeant. Much to his delight, Will received two letters. The first was from Mother, and he recognized her handwriting immediately. The second was from Mrs. McNabb. Will opened Mother's letter first.

Will,

I haven't heard from you, so I've been very worried that something might've happened to you. I haven't heard from your father either. I have some very sad news from Mrs. McNabb. Her husband, William, passed away in early June at the army hospital in Washington. He had been there for over a month from his injuries at somewhere near a place called Spotsylvania Courthouse in Virginia. I know you were there about the same time. Apparently, he was shot in the left arm, and I cannot imagine how much he must have suffered for a month. To compound her grief, the army told her that Mr. McNabb is being buried in a new cemetery across the river in Virginia. I don't quite understand it, but apparently it was the family estate or plantation for the General Lee family. It appears the North has confiscated it and turned it into a Union Army burial ground. It's so sad because Mrs. McNabb will probably never be able to travel that far to visit her husband's grave.

The children here are fine, and you will be proud that Albert has done a great job of planting the potatoes. His corn is already eight to ten inches high. He has learned to work the horses as well, and he's breaking the young team in at the same time.

He will start making hay this week if the weather holds. My, how wonderful it would be if you and Father were here all working together. I pray every night this terrible war will come to an end soon. The Butler Eagle *newspaper has stories every day with photographs by some man named Brady. I'm not sure how he does it and how he gets them delivered to the newspaper where they can publish them. Some of those photographs are very gruesome, and as a mother and wife, I can close my eyes and fearfully see you or your father injured and so far from home. Please take the time to drop me a note and let me know that you're doing fine.*

Love from your mother and all the youngsters at home.

Will realized he had been so caught up in his own problems with his wound that he had not taken a few moments to write to Mother. The army had realized it was a great morale builder if soldiers were able to send mail home, and so the government made it a free service. The government also knew that soldiers were in better spirits when they received mail from home, and so between the post office and the Department of War, the shipment of mail to the front became a priority.

Back at his tent, Will sat down to write a letter.

Dear Mother,

I just received your letter, and I am saddened by the loss of Mr. McNabb. My heart goes out to Mrs. McNabb, and to Laura, Sara, and little Billy. I know Mr. McNabb had only a few months left on his three-year enlistment. It's hard to believe that he survived the fearsome and awful battles at Antietam and Gettysburg last year and the year before, only to be shot here in Virginia.

I hope this war is over soon, and I want to visit with them in Kittanning as soon as I can, maybe on my way home. I am going to write to her, and I'm going to send her one month of my pay. I have also saved up three months of my pay to send to you.

I haven't seen Father lately as the 14th Cav has been off in a different direction.

I must share with you that I have a wound where a Rebel slashed at me with a saber and cut my thigh, but it is well healed up. The physician thinks I'll be back in action in three weeks, so that'll be late July. I didn't want to worry you when I was first injured, as so many men develop infections and fevers and die from their injuries.

There seems to be fighting every day here, as General Grant pushed hard to move south. It looks like General Lee is headed south to the city of Petersburg, Virginia. The poor Union infantrymen are up against veteran Confederate soldiers. Right before I was injured, we watched wave after wave of Union soldiers charge against a heavily fortified Rebel position. The fortification, we were told, was almost seven miles long. More than 20,000 Union soldiers were killed or wounded in three days.

We had over 15,000 of us cavalrymen dispatched to take a railroad station and the Trevilian Station. We were met by 10,000 Rebel riders, but we took the station. We stayed for a few days, and a lot of the troopers were engaged in tearing up railroad track for several miles.

It was during this battle that a Rebel standing on the ground on my blind side swung his saber at me and hit my right thigh, giving me a wound about ten inches long. Medics carried me on a stretcher to surgery within the railroad station. Harry Minteer had connections, and I was able to get almost immediate attention.

It was painful to have the surgeon explore my gash, clean it, and then stitch me up. But I am one of the fortunate ones who survived.

I thank you for your prayers, and I'm eager to see William A. and Father soon.

Please say hello to Albert and the little ones and tell him I'm proud of his farming skills.

Your loving son,

Will

20

Special Duty

The captain of Will's company ordered him to report to the commander's tent, so Will hobbled there on his crutches. The colonel looked up from his desk where he was writing orders. He asked about Will's injury, and Will explained what had happened, adding that he hoped to be back in the saddle in less than a month. Then, to Will's surprise, the colonel asked about his reading and writing skills.

As a youngster, Will had attended a one-room school and completed what was referred to as normal school, or eight grades. Most students did not go beyond the eight years, but Will was fortunate. He had been able to attend the West Sunbury Academy for a year. There, he learned basic penmanship and writing, along with philosophy, Latin, Greek, mathematics, and hygiene.

Will told him about attending the academy, so the colonel asked him to take a pen and write by copying orders that were already written out. Will quickly took a seat at a small desk and wrote out a duplicate set of orders. The colonel was pleased that Will's penmanship was legible and done quickly and neatly. He told Will that starting tomorrow morning, he was to report to the captain's tent and would be expected to write copies of orders and communications on behalf of the captain. Will felt delighted that he would be doing something other than sitting around camp.

Will spent the next three weeks working at the small table in the captain's tent. He enjoyed hearing the discussion among the officers and found it fascinating how they debated what the next moves would be for the cavalry and infantry. It seemed like orders were coming and going all day long, and Will was constantly busy writing them out.

One morning, a rider rode up with orders from General Grant and General Sheridan. Apparently, General Lee had retreated to the city of Petersburg. It was viewed as a delaying tactic to keep the Yankee army from heading to the capital of Richmond. Petersburg was well protected, and Lee's men were digging in and building fortifications. As Will transcribed the orders, he could see that General Grant was determined to continue sending masses of infantrymen against the Confederates, as it would take frontal attacks to break through. But first, the artillery would bombard the city of Petersburg. It was Grant's hope that General Lee would surrender. Other orders indicated that the cavalry would move against smaller targets, and that they were to try to shut off the city of Petersburg from any supplies coming in. Captured goods, livestock, and munitions would be returned to the Union lines. Troops also were to burn and destroy any means of production, such as cotton mills, mines, and fields.

Part of the orders from General Grant to General Sheridan were that the cavalry would be consolidated, and that General Sheridan would have forces under his command of twenty thousand cavalrymen and nineteen thousand infantrymen. Sheridan was charged with taking the city of Winchester, Virginia, a major crossroads of highways and railroad tracks. This city had been the gateway to the North. The Confederate Army on two prior occasions had moved north in the Shenandoah Valley and crossed into Maryland and threatened to cross into Pennsylvania.

Early in July 1864, Will was summoned to the company commander's tent. There, the colonel told him how much he had appreciated Will's penmanship and spelling as well as his speed in translating orders to be sent out to his subordinates.

"You've done such a good job that General Sheridan has requested that you be transferred temporarily to be his aide," the colonel told him. "You are to report tomorrow morning and in a clean uniform. Take your equipment and horse with you, as this assignment may last more than a few days. You're dismissed."

Will was dazed as he walked back to his tent and shared the news with Harry. Will had been looking forward to getting back into battle, although most of the assignments that were handed to the 4th Pennsylvania Cavalry now were skirmishes and scouting.

"Will, the good news is that you will be relatively safe from more injury, and we sure hope this war is over maybe yet this summer," Harry said. "As you know, General Grant is trying to outmaneuver General Lee, and it looks like we have the Confederates on the run. I think this is one of the best things that could have happened to you."

Will spent the afternoon going to the quartermaster's tent and picking up a new uniform, cleaning his gear, saddle, and tack, and making sure the black horse was groomed. The next morning, he arose early and reported right after breakfast to General Sheridan's quarters.

Short and stocky, General Philip Sheridan was also a man of action. He had once galloped his black stallion at full speed from Washington, D.C., for over fifty miles to Winchester, Virginia, to roust his troops and push the Confederates south. He had served under General Grant in Mississippi along with his great friend General William Tecumseh Sherman, who was leading an army across Georgia, cutting off Atlanta from the rest of the Confederacy.

Will was met by a captain, who interviewed him, and then when General Sheridan was ready, the captain presented Will to him as his new aide. "Son, I have been receiving back copies of my orders that you have transcribed," the general said. "I admire your handwriting and your ability to translate other people's writing accurately. I tend to write out my orders on the spot and make them short and to the point. I will need you to transcribe them quickly for me and make several copies to be dispatched promptly to our troops. Do I make myself clear?"

"Yes, sir," Will responded. "I am ready to serve and start immediately."

The captain showed Will to a small table inside the general's tent. He also told him to pitch a pup tent behind the general's tent so he could be summoned any hour of the day or night when the general was ready to give orders. He was further instructed to picket his black horse on the line where the officers had picketed. The captain told him that as soon as he had completed those chores to report back to headquarters.

Will was surprised when he came back to the general's tent and was taken aside by General Sheridan, who sat him down on a stump. "Son, tell me about yourself. How long have you been in this army? Have you seen any combat? Do you have any family serving under me? And what is the story on that black horse that you brought in with you?"

Will responded that he had joined the army last winter, he had trained in Harrisburg, and he had been in combat through the Wilderness, at Yellow Tavern and Appomattox Court House, and that he had been wounded in the battle at Trevilian Station. Will further shared that his uncle William A. was also in the 4th Pennsylvania Cavalry and that his father had been serving in the 14th Pennsylvania Cavalry since

November 1962. He also said he had brought the black horse from home, and they had been together all the way from the farm in Pennsylvania.

"Private, I want you to understand that everything you hear and read here is confidential. Do not share any information with anyone, including your uncle or your father. There are spies everywhere, and if word got out about our plans, many of your fellow Union soldiers could die because the enemy would be prepared and waiting for us. If you fail to obey this order, you could be court-martialed and executed by a firing squad. Is that clear and understood?"

Will was shaken by the order and the tone of General Sheridan, but he understood the severity of his responsibilities.

"Yes, sir!" Will responded. "Clearly understood, sir!"

For the next weeks, orders flowed from General Sheridan as he took command of over 39,000 troops. He organized the cavalry and put General George Armstrong Custer in charge of 20,000 mounted men and 19,000 support infantrymen. Since the Trevilian Station battle, the 4th Cavalry had engaged in skirmishes with Confederate cavalry now commanded by Major Wade Hampton and Major Fitzhugh Lee as replacements for the deceased General J. E. B. Stuart. The 4th had lost their commander, Colonel Covode, who had been injured in a fight at St. Mary's Church and died June 25. Samuel B. M. Young was promoted the same day to colonel in the 4th Cavalry.

General Grant's siege of the city of Saint Petersburg got underway at the end of June and lasted throughout July. Meanwhile, the 4th Cavalry was sent out scouting and in support of General Grant. They engaged in skirmishes at Charles Crossroads, Warwick Swamp, Malvern Hill, Deep Bottom along the James River, Gravel Hill, Strawberry Plains, and White Oak Swamp. About five hundred troops from the 4th Pennsylvania Cavalry were assigned to destroy the Walden Railroad. They also conducted reconnaissance to Poplar Springs Church and to Dinwiddie Court House. This kept them busy well into September 1864.

21

Black Horse

Will had not spent much time with the black horse while he had been recuperating and busy writing out orders for General Sheridan. But finally, a Sunday came when General Sheridan took a day away from headquarters to ride and see the troops. Will decided to spend some time with his steed, taking the black horse to the river to bathe and groom him.

As he curried out the horse, Will lifted the heavy black mane that hung down to the left side of his neck. Much to his dismay, the smell almost knocked Will over. Lifting the thick mane revealed a nasty wound along the black horse's neck. It was infected and had a horrific odor from pus and discharge.

Will tied the black horse to a sturdy oak tree along the riverbank and gently probed the wound with his pocketknife. More infected pus oozed out of the wound until the knife point struck a hard object. Will carefully inserted his forefinger into the wound. He felt the hard object and tried to grip it. Will figured it had to be a shell fragment or an object from an artillery shell. Many of the shells were loaded with grapeshot or shrapnel, so Will concluded that the black horse may have been hit several weeks ago, and his wound was hidden under the thick mane.

The black horse was nervous with the probing, but Will calmed him and took a break from the care. Will decided he needed to see Harry Minteer about how to possibly extract the fragment. Harry had been caring for horses since enlisting. Hurrying back to camp, Will found Harry, who had a long, slender set of tongs he had "borrowed" from the surgeon's office. Harry was able to get the tongs around a Minie ball that had burrowed two inches into the horse's neck. As the ball came out, so did a huge glob of infected flesh, blood, and pus. Harry wiped the wound clean and flushed it with a chemical fluid he had also procured from the surgeon's supplies.

Within a few days, a healthy pink color returned to the wound, indicating that the black horse was healing quickly after Harry's doctoring. Will felt thrilled that the horse was getting back to full health but chagrined at himself for having not discovered the wound earlier.

Will felt anxious to get back to riding with his company and the thrill of battle. He had grown bored sitting in General Sheridan's tent for long days on end copying and writing orders and occasionally riding out to deliver the orders.

The days were growing shorter, and each evening the temperatures dropped quickly as summer waned and fall rapidly approached. One evening, he was surprised as he finished his last transcription and heard William A. and Father approach the firepit near the tents. He had not seen either of them in several days.

William A. said his company had been riding daily, searching for Confederate troops and any movement by General Lee's troops. He said they seemed to have a skirmish every day and had taken several Rebel prisoners. William A. said most of the Rebs were suffering from malnutrition and wearing nothing but rags for uniforms, many of them barefoot, even the cavalrymen. They seemed almost eager to surrender in exchange for a good meal and a respite from the fight. Many of them were mentally defeated and knew the war was lost—only a matter of time before Lee surrendered the South.

Father added that his company had been riding and scouting to the northwest toward Winchester. He said he wouldn't be surprised if the Union would launch an attack in that direction. Scouting reports indicated that there was a large contingent of Confederates dug in and fortified on the hills northeast of Winchester. For now, the Rebels were in control of the gateway to the Shenandoah Valley and the city.

22

Off to Winchester

In early September, General Grant issued a detailed set of orders to General Sheridan. He was to send a division of Union cavalry and two corps of infantry to attack the Rebel positions near Winchester from the east. General Averell's cavalry and an additional cavalry division, including the 14th Pennsylvania Cavalry, were to attack from the north. They were up against Confederate General Earley's army of fifteen thousand men.

As Will transcribed the orders, it was clear this was going to be a major attack on a Confederate stronghold. General Custer was the leader of the cavalry on the Union's right flank, and under him was Colonel Schoonmaker of the 14th Pennsylvania Cavalry.

General Sheridan's instructions were to take the left flank of the Confederacy and charge it. General Sheridan was specific that all cavalrymen should have their sabers in the air and wave them in the sunlight. They should charge as hard as they could into the Confederate lines to intimidate the enemy soldiers. General Sheridan was sure that the Confederates were low on ammunition and food, and battle weary.

Part of the Union strategy was to take the end of the left flank of the Confederates by storm and get in behind their dug-in positions. Once the federal cavalry achieved this goal, they could ride down the lines shooting into the backs of the Confederate soldiers who had been dug in awaiting Union troops advancing in front of them. Fort Star stood on the north-west end of the Confederate line. General Averell ordered the 14th Pennsylvania Cavalry to charge the hill and take the fort.

⸺ ∽∾∾ ⸺

Father rode in Company M of the 14th. In his nearly three years of fighting, he had been involved in numerous skirmishes and battles. His first two years were mostly as a scout, but under the command of General Grant, the cavalry had become a fighting unit.

As the attack progressed, Andrew saw his captain, James K. Duncan, shot and mortally wounded on their way up against Fort Star. He saw several of his fellow riders get injured or have their horses shot out from under them in this brief but brutal attack against the fort. As they approached the dug-in enemy, Andrew and his fellow troopers charged at full speed across the last fifty yards of land, jumping over the fences and the defensive positions to get in behind the Rebels.

The 14th Cavalry managed to roll up the Confederate lines and sent the Confederate soldiers running on foot south through Winchester. More than four hundred of them were captured and taken prisoner and marched back behind Union lines. This was the last time during the Civil War that the Confederates would hold the town of Winchester.

As it turned out, this was the last great cavalry battle of the Civil War. From the middle of September when this battle was over until the end of 1864, there were numerous skirmishes as the Union cavalry chased the Confederates south and as the Union cavalry continued to seize crops and livestock and burn barns throughout Virginia on their march south toward Richmond, the Confederate capital.

Due to his role as an aide to General Sheridan, Will was kept in the rear of the action. The general was in charge, issuing commands and orders to the troops as they made the attacks. Will hastily transcribed the orders so they could be ridden off to commanders in the field. For the final assault, General Sheridan rode his black horse in the lead and was one of the first to jump over the Rebel picket lines. Will felt disappointed that he was not able to join the action because of his orders to stand by and assist at field headquarters.

Later, Will would describe his circumstances to Mother.

Dear Mother,

My wound has healed almost completely, but General Sheridan would not release me to active combat for a major battle for the cavalry. I'm anxious to see Father and William A. as they both were off to Winchester.

Troops tell me it was a beautiful September morning, sun shining off the sabers and rifles, and a terrific and hard-fought charge against a fort at the top of the hill. The 14th PA Cav led the charge and sent the Rebels running south through the streets of Winchester. I sure wish I could have been there on the black horse. He suffered a wound with a ball that struck him in the left side of his neck. I did not discover it right away, but Harry Minteer knew exactly what to do to extract the ball and help heal the wound.

General Sheridan shared with his command that he does not think the war will be over this fall as the siege of Petersburg is going quite slowly. Apparently, the command had hoped the Confederates would realize they were beaten, but they are sure determined, I give them that.

There is some talk that if the war is going to drag over to next spring, many of us may be getting a month's leave this winter. Most of the troops seem to think it will be based on seniority, so I may not be eligible, but it sure would be nice if Father and William A. could get home.

Please share my love with the children, and I am anxious to see you soon.

Love,

Your faithful son, Will

23

The Big Raid

After the battle of the Third Winchester, orders came down, and Will, much to his surprise, was released from his duties as aide to General Sheridan. He returned to Company A, excited that he might again ride into combat as the Union Army headed toward Richmond. The Confederates were in slow retreat to the south, as they were running out of food, ammunition, horses, and the will to continue the battle.

Will wrote to keep his mother informed:

Mother,

We have not yet been told where we will be going into winter quarters, but we suspect that we will start a spring campaign as early as possible, hopefully finishing this war before next summer. Frequently, we are sent out as a company of a hundred troopers, and we seem to spend more time foraging than fighting. Much as I hate it, we frequently destroy farms and burn the barns after we've taken the livestock and any grain and hay that we can carry off. We're helping to sustain our army at the same time as hoping to deprive the Confederates of the resources to continue the battle. Some of these barns are beautiful and have probably been around for more than a hundred years.

A lot of this country was at one time planted in cotton, but that played out the soil. Several of the farms are owned by the Amish or by German immigrants. While they don't seem to have an active role in the war, they have been supplying the Confederates all along. They do protest a lot when we arrive, but they do not believe in guns, and they do not show armed resistance. I sometimes think how awful it would be if this was reversed and a Confederate force was on your doorstep in Pennsylvania. But orders are orders, so I guess we do as told here in the army.

I get to spend more time in the evenings around campfires, or I chat with Harry Minteer, and I get to see Father frequently. He's looking good, but his hair has turned much whiter than I remember it when he left for the war back in 1861. He looks fit, and the 14th PA Cav also is lightly engaged in the Valley doing much the same as we're doing.

I miss you all back home, and I'm anxious to be home as soon as possible.

Your loving son, William

As November waned, Will could feel each day getting a little crisper and each night a little colder. The heavy rains from earlier in the month had abated somewhat. The sergeant came by mid-afternoon on the last day of November and told Will that his company should report for roll call at 4:00 p.m. on the main field. He said Company B would also be called up as well as two companies from the 14th Pennsylvania Cavalry.

Will felt excited, because sitting around camp had been boring, and he hoped that the assembly would mean an assignment. He quickly calculated that four companies would be about four hundred cavalrymen being called together. Promptly at 4:00 p.m., the commanding officer called the troops to attention, and General Sheridan rode up on his black horse to address the men.

"Men," he said, "we will be riding out at dawn tomorrow on a tough mission and a very hard ride. We will need to cover more than fifty miles overnight and across a ridge of mountains into enemy territory. Your company commander will now address you as you break out into your four companies."

The company commander told them all to secure seven days of oats for their horses, seven days of rations for themselves, a hundred rounds of ammunition, and to prepare to dress warmly. All troopers had been issued a heavy overcoat that came down almost to their ankles and up around their chins. It was split in the back so that riders could mount a saddle easily. Once mounted, the tail of the coat would drape over top of the saddlebags and bedroll to protect them from rain or snow.

Will was excited now to know they were going off on a hard ride, and he knew that the black horse would be raring to go as well. Will quickly rounded up everything he needed from the commissary and from the quartermaster. He fed the horse and then checked him over from nose to tail to make sure everything was fine with the horse. He then gathered up all his equipment, tack, and arms.

Will would enter the battle with more firearms than most of his contemporaries. He carried two .44 caliber pistols on his hips and two more .44 caliber Colt pistols in a pommel-mount set of holsters. On top of that, he had his .44 caliber carbine in a scabbard.

Back at his tent, he checked his saddle and saddlebags and cleaned them. He also wiped down all his weapons with a light oil. Next, he pulled out an extra set of underwear and socks and his only remaining shirt. He intended to layer up with all of them because he anticipated it would be a cold ride wherever they were going.

Once Will had finished his routine and preparation, he went over and found his father in Company M of the 14th Pennsylvania Cavalry. Will was excited that for the first time since he had entered his service last winter, he and Father would ride together under one command and close to each other. He asked his father if he knew where they were going. Father responded that he'd heard they were making a raid on a railroad facility, but that's all he knew.

Will still had time before evening chow, so he sat down and wrote to Mother to share with her that they were going off on a raid of some sort and that he was going to ride with Father. While they had both been engaged at the Winchester battle, they had been nowhere close to each other. So this would be the first time they might be in proximity.

Throughout the night, Will could hardly sleep in anticipation of the coming morning. He was wide awake long before the bugle sounded to roust the troops. Will quickly saddled up the black horse, loaded his gear, pommel saddlebags and rear saddlebags, strapped on his carbine, then rolled his bedroll and secured it behind the cantle on his McClelland saddle. He fed the black horse with a nose bag full of a quart of oats. While the horse feasted, Will headed to the mess tent and grabbed a cup of coffee, two sausage biscuits, and a slice of fresh bread. There were two hundred soldiers from the 4th Cavalry all doing the same thing, and he could hear across the field the same kind of noise coming from the 14th Pennsylvania Cavalry as they prepared for the ride too.

All around him the troopers were untying their horses from their picket lines and heading to the assembly field to line up by company and squad. Will quickly found his place in Company A, and he could see behind him that Company B was forming up as well. Just as the sun peeked over the top of the mountains in the Shenandoah Valley, officers were instructing each company to get ready.

Finally came the command to form up in columns of four abreast and move out. They set a quick pace at a light trot and stayed in formation across the western side of the Shenandoah Valley for three hours, and after a short break, they started to move up a valley into the mountains to the west of them. They stopped at noon for a fifteen-minute respite. They were near a stream, so the men watered their horses and filled their canteens.

After the noon break, instructions came to mount up but now to ride two abreast as the passageway was getting narrower up the first set of hills that they encountered. While they were not in a trot, they were still at a fast walk and making good time. Will was concerned as the sky to the west had become cloudy and the temperature seemed to be dropping. By mid-afternoon, a slight drizzle had started. That made the footing a little slipperier for the horses, and the men pulled their topcoats tight around their necks, making sure that the tails of their coats covered the saddlebags as best they could. Right before dark, around five p.m., the command called a halt, and again the men took a short break. This time they enjoyed some of their sausage biscuits and hardtack provisions and gave their horses their nose bag full of oats for the second feeding of the day.

When the men remounted, they stayed in columns of two and started up a much steeper trail that was especially difficult now that it was dark. The drizzle continued, and from time to time the rain got heavier. While the greatcoats protected the riders, they also absorbed a lot of rainwater and weighed heavily across the shoulders of the troopers. It seemed like they were forever crossing a creek and headed up the other side, and then in a half hour or so they would head back down the far side of that ridge and come to another creek. At each creek the horses were offered an opportunity to drink so that they stayed hydrated.

Sometime around midnight, the troops halted, and the sergeant rode back past each squad. He told them that the next climb would be extremely steep on switchback trails and that they would cross a deep creek several times. He said the men should reach up and grab the tail of the horse in front of them and not let go, enabling them all to stay on the same trail in the dark.

Will was glad he had packed the extra pair of gloves and donned his extra shirt, an extra pair of long underwear, and the extra pair of socks. He was surprised how difficult it was to hold on to the tail of the horse in front of him but glad to have a point of reference. Otherwise, he would have been completely lost in what seemed to be pitch-black darkness all around him. It took two more hours until they had crested the ridge and dropped down the far side of it, still holding on to the horse in front.

Finally, at three a.m., the sergeant came back and said they had reached the valley and would grab three or four hours of sleep while they could. He warned everybody that they were deep into enemy territory. The men were exhausted because they had now been in the saddle for more than twenty hours, covering somewhere between fifty and a hundred miles.

As they dismounted, the sergeant told them to leave the saddles on their horse and to tie a lead rope to the halter of their horse and hold it in one hand if they were going to lie down and try to sleep. It seemed like no time at all before the troopers were on the ground trying to fall asleep. Although it was cold and raining and the ground was soaking wet, the men stretched out, each with a hand on their horse's lead rope.

The temperature had been steadily dropping all throughout the night. Will couldn't see much, but it felt like the rain had turned to snow when he lay down. Still, in a matter of minutes, he was sound asleep. The wind had stopped, but snowfall dropped over six inches of new snow on top of the sleeping cavalrymen.

Shortly before dawn, the sergeant was up and about, soon ordering the bugler to sound revelry. He got a big chuckle out of watching the troopers pop up out of the snow and look around in disbelief. One trooper called out that he needed help. Turns out he had exceptionally long hair, and when he lay down, it froze in the mud before the snow covered them all up. Will and another trooper used their knives to cut some of his hair loose so he could sit up, and they all had a good laugh about it.

In a few minutes the troops were assembled in the open pasture where they had spent the night, and they still had a way to go, according to the command. Once again, they rode out in columns of four, but the men were instructed to have their rifles out of the scabbards and across their arms in case of attack. Advanced scouts had ridden out in front and along the edges of their trail, not spotting any enemy. The sergeant informed them they had crossed into Tennessee and that they were headed to a major railroad junction.

Around ten a.m., they crested the last ridge and could look down over a river valley. Along the edge of the river valley were a set of railroad tracks running east to west and another set of railroad tracks that met them that ran to the south. Word spread that this was a major supply line for the Confederate Army, and the cavalry's mission was to destroy as much of the railroad as it could in a short period of time.

When they reached the edge of the rail track, the four hundred men were divided into different commands. Because Will was such a crack shot with a rifle, he was sent to a high point along with nine other troopers to serve as lookouts. They were told that if they spotted enemy movement, they should engage the Confederates as quickly as possible to cause a distraction. This mission was to do their damage and get back out safely.

Meanwhile, most of the troopers were sent in all four directions on the railroad track with sets of crowbars, shovels, and sledgehammers. Their instructions were to tear up the rail line ties, stack them as high as they could, and then stack the rails against the ties. The plan was to set each stack on fire, and the heat of the burning railroad ties would help melt the rails and bend them so that they would not be useful for the reconstruction of the rail lines later. The soldiers would not light any of the fires until they had destroyed as much railroad as they could, and then they would ignite all the pyramids as fast as they could and ride east back into Virginia.

As they worked feverishly, all the guards on the hills were on high alert, knowing that the activity, noise, and eventually the smoke from the fires would draw attention from whatever Confederate troops were nearby. Will knew that the Rebels had been moving south in Virginia, but he wasn't sure they'd had much pressure from Union forces here in Tennessee.

A few times, Will thought he spotted movement off in the distance, but each time it turned out not to be Confederate soldiers. The activity was either cows in a far-off field or horses out to pasture at nearby farms. As the hardworking troopers moved farther away from the junction of the two railroads, they became more vulnerable, so the guards were doubled up to give protection to those troopers farthest from the intersection.

By three p.m., the commanding officers convened and decided it was time to head back over the mountains before dark. They had a string of mules that had followed the four hundred troopers, hauling needed equipment and more than two hundred gallons of kerosene.

The troopers were instructed to douse each pyramid of ties and rails with kerosene. As soon as they had a good fire going on one of them, they would take firebrands to the next one and light it. With the piles ignited in quick succession, the soldiers would move back to the junction, where the two roads met. When the troops were reassembled, they would all hightail it out to the east. It took about an hour for the farthest troops who lit their pyramids to work their way back to the gathering point. By now the sky was full of black smoke, but fortunately, clouds had rolled in again, so the smoke was not clearly visible.

Within a half hour, the wind shifted, and with it, the dark plumes of smoke from the burning railroad ties billowed high into the sky like a signal flare. Will stood up in his stirrups, scanning the horizon. His eyes narrowed.

"Riders," he muttered. "Southbound."

A flicker of movement caught his attention beyond the haze—mounted men in gray and riding hard toward them, a dust trail curling behind.

"Cavalry patrol! South on the run!" Will barked, lifting his rifle.

The sergeant spun in the saddle and shouted, "To arms! Form a line! You boys know what to do!"

Troopers scrambled, boots pounding the dirt as they grabbed rifles and took up firing positions along the rise overlooking the tracks. Ten bluecoats braced against the wind, rifles ready, smoke curling between them like a restless ghost.

"Steady, boys. Steady now," the sergeant called out, his voice low and calm as a drawn blade. "Let 'em come in closer."

The oncoming Confederate riders slowed, their mounts tossing their heads as they reached the edge of the smoldering track. Clearly, they had seen the smoke—maybe even smelled the creosote and scorched iron—and they knew what it meant: destruction.

The Rebel patrol hesitated, riders bunching up, weapons raised but unsure. Will tightened his grip on the Henry, heart pounding like a drum in his chest. The lead scout stood tall in the saddle, glassing the Union position with a spyglass.

"They're gonna bolt," Will whispered.

"Take 'em!" the sergeant shouted.

Crack-crack-crack! The line erupted in gunfire. Will sighted in and fired—his round slammed into the lead scout's chest, knocking him backward out of the saddle. Another Rebel horse toppled, throwing its rider. Across the field, men fell and horses reared and scattered in chaos.

"Reload! Reload!" someone shouted.

Smoke from the rifles joined that from the fires, turning the field into a grim, ghostly haze.

The remaining Confederates wheeled about in panic, riding hard for the hills. But not fast enough—Union bullets found their mark. Two more saddles emptied before they were out of range.

"Mount up!" came the new order.

"Every man for himself—head east!"

There was no formation now—just a blur of motion, hooves thundering as troopers raced to escape before a larger Rebel force responded. Will slapped a new cartridge into his Henry, racked it, and slung it across his back. He glanced around—most of the demolition troops had already scattered.

He spun the horse around, gripping the reins tight. "Let's go, boy!"

The stallion surged forward, and within moments, Will was galloping past stragglers, dodging brush and downed trees, the wind tearing at his coat as he chased down the main body of the cavalry. He caught up and rejoined his company.

They rode hard for two hours, the burning tracks long behind them, the land falling into shadow as dusk crept across the mountains. The thunder of hooves finally slowed when a sharp whistle signaled a halt.

"Hold up! Dismount and water your mounts!"

Will slid from the saddle, wincing as he hit the ground. His thigh still throbbed from the old wound, but he pushed through it, leading the black horse to a nearby creek, where he drank deeply.

Nearby, troopers collapsed to the ground, breathing hard, their faces streaked with soot and sweat. Someone passed a tin cup of water, and someone else chewed absently on a biscuit, their eyes half-closed in exhaustion.

Will reached into his saddlebag and pulled out a chunk of hardtack. He said to the trooper beside him, "It's cold as stone and hard as a rock, but it's all we got."

"Right now," the other man responded, "it'll fill an empty stomach, and that's good enough."

As the shadows deepened, the captain rode down the line, voice raised. "Listen up! We're not staying here. We ride all night—back over the ridge. If there's a Rebel force on the way, we'll be long gone by the time they arrive."

Groans rippled through the line, but no one protested. The soldiers were too tired to argue, too seasoned to complain. They knew the mission had been a success. The Confederate supply line was in ashes, and General Sheridan would be pleased.

Will looked to the horizon where the last light was fading. He rubbed his leg, tired to the bone but satisfied.

"We'll make it," the trooper beside him said.

Will nodded. "Yeah. One more ride. Then we'll sleep in the valley . . . and wait for winter."

The bugle sounded the signal. One by one, the troopers mounted up, and the long, silent column began to move—vanishing into the night like ghosts of smoke and iron.

24

Headed Home

In early December, the bugles sounded assembly. It was a surprise to Will and probably to all the cavalrymen who had been getting ready for winter quarters. Under the command of General Sheridan, they had taken over a large railroad station and surrounding warehouses and set up a good camp with everybody now sleeping under a roof as winter approached.

Once all the troopers were lined up on the assembly field, General Sheridan addressed them. He thanked them for their service, and many would be granted furloughs based on time and service. He said that the company commanders and the sergeants of each squad would have the details available immediately. He wished safe journeys to all of those who were traveling and said he felt confident that they were going to put an end to this war in the early part of 1865.

The furloughs were for those who had more than one year of service. Will knew he was not eligible, but he was elated that his father, who hadn't been home in two years, would likely get a nice furlough along with William A. As soon as Will was dismissed from the squad, he walked over to the 14th Pennsylvania Cavalry and found his father.

Andrew told his son he had been granted a thirty-day leave plus two days of travel time on either end of his leave. William A. was also granted the same. They were busy packing, as they were told they might depart as early as that evening. Will shared with his father that he wanted to send his love home to Mother and his siblings and let them know how much he would miss being with them for Christmas. Soon, orders came down for those on leave to depart on a train that evening for Washington, D.C.

When the soldiers arrived in D.C. late at night, officers stood at every station directing the men to a large warehouse adjacent to the train station. There, orderlies rushed about with buckets of hot water. The soldiers were ordered to strip, bathe, and wash their hair. This was no luxury experience, as the temperature was in the thirty-degree range, but the men quickly bathed and dried their hair. An orderly then checked their hair for lice and other critters. They were issued new long underwear and uniforms, and their old clothes were gathered to be burned.

Next, the soldiers were lined up in chairs and had their hair cut much shorter. They were also offered either a trim of their beards or a complete shave. Once they were shorn, clothed in new uniforms, and ready for presentation, an officer quickly inspected each of them and then ordered them to the train station. At the station, they were met by a transportation specialist who directed them to their assigned train units and departure times.

For Andrew and William A., their departure was sched- uled for ten p.m. on Track 3, and they were told to report at eight p.m. They decided to see if there was a shop where they could buy little gifts for their spouses and kids at home. Andrew decided that Mother would love to have some lace, silk, and perhaps needles and thread. He was able to pick those up for her, and for each of the girls at home he found small stuffed dolls that he put into his haversack. He purchased a knife with a carved handle and sheath for Albert.

Andrew and William A. decided they'd better find some- thing to eat. Among the many vendors at the rail station, they selected one selling pork sausages, beans, and canned peaches. The latter was a great treat as they had not had anything like that since before the war. They decided to stuff a couple of sausages in their haversacks so they would have something to eat during their journey.

Andrew suggested that they board early and try to find seats in the middle of the car so they would be away from the windows and doors blowing in cold air. Andrew knew the car would be overloaded and some men would either sleep on the floor or stand all night for the trip.

Around eight p.m., other troopers started to load the train and by nine it was packed with every seat taken. The train did not pull out at ten o'clock as scheduled, but around midnight they felt the tug of the engine starting to move the cars, rolling out of Washington, D.C., and headed west. Soon they were out in open country, and it seemed like the train might have been doing as much as thirty miles per hour. They had been told that there were two engineers on board and two sets of crews all ready to make a nonstop trip to Pittsburgh. Shortly before noon the following day, they rolled into Pittsburgh and unloaded.

William A. and his family lived in Butler, and Andrew's family lived ten miles north of Butler. They had discussed on the way from Washington, D.C., how they were going to proceed north.

At the train station, they were told about stagecoaches that ran all the way from Pittsburgh to Erie with a stop in Butler. At the stagecoach ticket office, they were told that a stage would be leaving at two p.m. and would make it to Butler late that evening. They decided to splurge and buy tickets at fifty cents apiece to ride the stage.

Andrew had slept a bit during the night on the train, but after daylight he was wide awake and pondering his return. His wife and children had no idea he was on his way home, so it would come as a big surprise. The short notice of leave had not given the men time to write home. He was especially anxious to see what little Priscilla looked like. She had been born in 1858, and when he first left for war, she was only four years old. He wondered whether she would remember him. He tried to imagine if Albert had grown as much over the last two years as Will had.

Andrew eagerly anticipated being home over Christmas. He was already making plans to find a nice pine tree to bring into the house and put everyone in the sleigh for the ride to church in West Sunbury on Christmas morning.

⸺ ◦◦◦◦ ⸺

William A. and Andrew made their way to the boarding area for the stagecoach to Butler. The coach was designed to hold six passengers on the top out in the open and six passengers inside the cabin. It cost more money to be inside the coach than on top of it. Up front, the driver sat on the right side holding the reins for his team of four horses, and on the left front was a guard armed with a double-barreled .10-gauge shotgun.

Having ridden a stagecoach many times before, Andrew motioned to William A. that they should board first. Up top, they took the last row of seats, and they each took the outside of the last row. In that position, the passengers in front of them would serve as a windbreak against the December gusts that were coming off Lake Erie with bone-chilling effect.

The departure was on time, and the driver announced that the roads were good, no big mudholes, and the plank road portion was where they would make good time. As they boarded the coach, Andrew noticed he and William A. were the only ones in uniform. Two well-dressed couples had boarded the coach along with two dapper businessmen. They filled the main lower enclosed coach cabin.

The four men up top with Andrew and William A. were rough-dressed men, probably in their thirties. As Andrew listened to their conversations, he decided these were the oilmen Will had described. Their clothes smelled of petroleum, and they talked of drilling and the hard work ahead. For whatever reason, Andrew assumed they were likely all armed with pistols and knives, a thought that gave him some comfort as he was unarmed for the first time in years, having been required to leave his weapons in camp while on leave.

The driver handed out robes to those on top. He said once the sun dipped over the western skyline, it would get cold. The guard stood in his position in the front.

Andrew pulled his greatcoat up around his neck. He decided he would spend the night in Butler and then early tomorrow walk or catch a ride to the farm, about ten miles north. He decided he'd splurge and get a bath and shave on Main Street first thing in the morning so he would be as well presented as he could be. It had been over two years since he had slept in a bed or even in a house.

25

Roadside Robbery

Before he climbed aboard the stage, the driver shouted to the passengers that it was a forty-mile trip to Butler. He said they would be stopping at a halfway point at a tavern called the Dixon Inn. The inn would provide a light meal, probably soup, homemade bread, and coffee. He told them they would switch teams that would already be harnessed and ready to go. The four horses that got them halfway there would be rested, and four new horses would take them the last half of the trip. He said part of the road was called the Plank Highway because a long stretch had boards laid down to help with efficient travel. The driver also pointed out that there had been a string of stagecoach robberies recently, and he wanted everyone to be on alert.

"Gentlemen, if you carry, please be ready to join in if highwaymen attempt to bushwhack us," the driver said. "You men on top, there are fifteen-shot Henry rifles hidden along the outside rail on top of the coach. Use them if needed."

The first part of the trip was pleasant as the afternoon sun warmed the riders through the heavy clothes, but as the sun started to dip on the western sky, the temperatures dropped quickly. Andrew knew this route, having traveled it several times. Soon, he nodded off and dreamt of being home by tomorrow. He was jerked awake by the slowing of the coach, and he could see dim lights ahead, likely the Dixon Inn.

A team of four horses and a coach pulled out and headed south to Pittsburgh. The two drivers stopped and chatted for a few minutes and exchanged information about the road conditions ahead for both.

Finally, as they approached the inn, Andrew saw a team of four horses, harnessed and waiting to be hooked up to the stage. Across the road were three dismounted riders, holding the reins of their mounts. As the driver stopped the team and set the brakes, he told all the passengers they should plan on a twenty-minute stop, and they would find the necessary facilities behind the tavern.

⚬⚬⚬

Darkness crept over the trees like a slow-moving storm as Andrew climbed back onto the coach, his boots thudding softly against the wooden step. The warm glow of the tavern lanterns cast long, flickering shadows across the dusty yard.

From atop the coach, Andrew spotted the three riders again—now mounted, watching. One sat tall in fringed buckskin, his rifle no longer tucked away but resting across his saddle, his right hand on the stock and his left arm bent at an odd angle. The other two, dressed in ragged homespun clothes and slouch hats, looked no less dangerous, their horses pawing restlessly at the dirt.

Something was wrong.

Andrew leaned toward William A. and the oilmen boarding behind him, keeping his voice low. "They're still out there—and one's drawn a rifle. Keep your weapons close and ready. Don't move unless I say."

The oil workers nodded, quietly gripping their weapons and checking their loads. William A. moved toward one of the Henry rifles, eyes fixed on the riders.

Outside, the coach driver and the guard were preoccupied, tightening hitches and adjusting the fresh team of four horses for the run to Butler. Neither noticed the riders shifting in their saddles.

From the tavern's front door, the wealthier passengers emerged laughing and chatting, unaware of the danger creeping toward them. A lady in a bonnet clutched her parasol, while a rotund merchant wiped his mustache and adjusted his pocket watch.

Then it happened.

Two of the rough-looking riders suddenly dismounted. Steel flashed in the dimming light—pistols drawn. One stepped forward, voice cutting through the quiet like a whip crack.

"Hands up! This is a robbery!"

The second followed, waving a sack. "Empty your pockets! Jewelry, watches, gold—into the bag, now!"

The passengers froze in terror. The merchant dropped his watch with a clatter.

The stagecoach guard spun to react—but too late. One of the robbers leveled a pistol straight at him. The guard's double-barreled shotgun lay useless, propped against the coach wheel just out of reach.

The rider in buckskin began trotting forward, rifle high, his eyes scanning for threats.

From his place on top of the coach, Andrew's voice was barely audible. "Wait . . . not yet . . . hold steady."

He watched the robbers move among the passengers, waving their weapons. One slapped a man when he hesitated to hand over his valuables. A woman whimpered and tossed a velvet pouch into the sack.

Andrew's heart pounded. "On my count," he hissed, hand clenched on the Henry rifle. "Three . . . two . . . one—now!"

William A. and the oilmen raised their rifles and fired almost as one. The shots rang out in sharp cracks, echoing off the tavern walls.

The first robber stumbled backward, arms flailing before he crashed into the dirt. The second tried to run but was cut down in a volley, his pistol tumbling from his hand as he collapsed.

Andrew swung his Henry rifle toward the rider in buckskin. The man's eyes widened—too late.

Andrew squeezed the trigger. The .44 round slammed into the rider's chest, knocking him sideways in the saddle. Andrew fired again—another flash, another hit. The third shot struck somewhere between horse and rider as the animal bucked wildly. With a strangled grunt, the rider slid to the ground in a heap.

Silence fell, broken only by the snorting of spooked horses and the ragged breathing of passengers.

The stagecoach guard retrieved his shotgun and walked toward the fallen robbers, nudging them with the toe of his boot. "Stone cold," he muttered. "Both of 'em."

The driver hurriedly checked on the passengers. "Anyone hurt?"

They shook their heads, eyes wide.

"Not bad for oilmen," the guard said, glancing at the armed workers, then over to Andrew. "You led that well, mister."

Andrew didn't respond. He was already walking toward the buckskin-clad man, who lay in the dirt, blood staining the front of his coat.

"Hold up," said the guard, kneeling beside the rider. "He's still breathin'."

The two men hauled the wounded man to the porch of the tavern and laid him across a thick table under the awning. Blood pooled beneath him as his breaths grew ragged.

Andrew stood over him, rifle still in hand. The man blinked slowly, lips moving in a whisper.

"You'll live long enough to answer questions," Andrew said coldly.

The buckskin man coughed, blood speckling his chin. "Wasn't supposed to go this way . . ."

Behind him, the passengers gathered in a silent circle, the flickering lamplight catching the fear still etched in their faces.

"Let's hope not many more plan to make it go that way," Andrew said, turning away and scanning the tree line once more.

The night had fallen hard—but the danger hadn't passed just yet.

⬥

This brazen attempt to rob the stage was big news. The stationmaster telegraphed the county sheriff, who wired back that he was less than ten miles away and would come right away. In a few minutes, a southbound stage pulled in, and as luck would have it, there was a medical doctor on board. He had been in Butler performing surgery and had his equipment bag with him for his trip home to Pittsburgh.

Lanterns were hung above the table, and the buckskin shirt was cut back to reveal the wounds. A probe of the chest shot revealed a hole straight through the chest, missing the heart and exiting out of the back. The second shot had passed through muscle on the upper left arm and again did not hit any bone.

The doctor gave the patient morphine and stitched up and bandaged his wounds. Then the stationmaster and the guard carried the wounded man to a back room in the tavern. The guard posted himself outside the door awaiting the arrival of the sheriff.

All the passengers were told to return to the tavern as they would need to talk to the sheriff when he arrived. Meanwhile, the stationmaster covered the bodies of the two dead robbers next to the stagecoach.

When the sheriff arrived, he took about an hour to talk to the passengers and to question the driver, guard, oil workers, and finally William A. and Andrew. He then gathered them all around and said they had been looking for this gang, which had been robbing passengers in this area. He would report that the robbers were shot while in the act of robbery, and no charges would be filed against any passengers. He said he would take charge of the prisoner and, as soon as he was able, take him to the jail in Butler. He got the addresses of all passengers so they might be summoned as witnesses at a trial. The sheriff also made a list of all the items that the passengers had put in the robbers' gunny sack and then returned the goods to the passengers.

With that, they were dismissed. The driver had everyone reboard so he could get back onto the Plank Highway and head to Butler, although two hours behind schedule and running in full darkness. As a safety precaution, he lit and hung two lanterns on the front of the cabin of the stage so others could see him coming, as he intended to run this team hard to make up for lost time.

The night air was filled by the shouts of the driver as he called out to the team and pushed them hard. They had twenty miles to cover in the dark, but they were helped by the bright light of a nearly full moon. The team galloped along, slowed only when they came to some of the steeper grades they had to climb.

At long last, they descended the final hill into Butler, past the glowing fires of the furnaces of an ironworks on the west side of the road, and rounded the last curve before crossing the new iron bridge on Main Street. Finally, they pulled up in front of the Diamond Street Square. There stood the county courthouse, the stagecoach corral and station, and two hotels. The clock on the courthouse showed just past ten o'clock—not bad given their delay.

Much to the surprise of all the passengers, a reporter for the *Butler Eagle* newspaper was waiting for them. He had apparently been alerted by the sheriff's office of the attempted robbery, maybe from the telegraph wire that had been sent from the Dixon Inn. He first approached the driver and guard for details of the holdup and shootings, and they shared that the soldiers and oil workers had saved the day by opening fire on the armed highwaymen.

When the reporter asked William A. for his name and details, he shared his name of William A. Eshenbaugh and his brother Andrew as the soldiers. He told the reporter he did not know the names of the oil field workers who had also opened fire, but the reporter seemed far more interested in a story about the two soldiers on their way home from the war and their role of foiling the robbery. Andrew told the reporter he did not have anything to add—they just did their duty.

The next morning, the headline in the *Eagle* read, "Soldiers Kill Highway Robbers." The article offered a detailed account of the shootings, with the names of all involved. Andrew and William A. had decided to check into the hotel across the square the night before, and when they came down to breakfast, diners arose to give them a round of applause. The innkeeper told them their breakfast and room were on the house for their service to the Union and their bravery with the stagecoach shootout. Andrew and William A. were stunned and wanted no part of being heroes but grateful for the warm reception.

Both were anxious to get on home but went to get a haircut, clean shave, and a bath at the hotel before heading out. An hour later, William A. and Andrew shook hands and agreed to meet back here for the stage to Pittsburgh on January 2. With that, William A. headed down the street to his home.

26

Home at Last

Andrew headed north on Main Street, determined to walk the ten miles to his farm if he could not hitch a ride. At the north end of Butler, a long, steep hill led out of town. At the bottom of the hill was a watering trough. When Andrew reached it, there was a farmer with a load of supplies taking care of his team. Andrew greeted him, and the farmer asked him if he was home on furlough or had finished his enlistment. Andrew shared that he was on leave and his enlistment would run into late 1865.

The farmer asked where he was headed, and Andrew said his home was a farm about a mile south of West Sunbury.

"You are in luck today, my friend," said the farmer. "I'm headed to the feed mill in West Sunbury to deliver a load of supplies, so hop on the wagon."

Andrew could not believe his good fortune, as this meant he would be dropped off right in front of his home.

Just before noon, the team topped the last hill before Andrew's farm, and soon he caught sight of his house and barn. What a welcome sight—the sight of home and family and all he loved and had been fighting for since 1861.

When the wagon came to a halt at the end of his lane, Andrew stepped down from the wagon and thanked the farmer for the ride. As the team pulled away, Andrew stood at the top of his lane and took in the view. Before him stood his home, the house he had built with the bank barn beyond it, the wagon shed, corn crib, hen house, the pump and well, and even the outhouse. All were so familiar, and all held so many memories of what this land looked like before he settled it. He recalled all the labor it took to clear the land, build the buildings, and make it a home. He whiffed the air and smelled the smoke from the hearth fire.

Suddenly, the door opened, and a young girl ran to the dinner bell and rang it hard and loud. Out of the woods beyond the barn came a team and a wagon loaded with firewood and driven by Albert, headed in for dinner as the noontime meal was called. Andrew smiled to himself. What good fortune to arrive just in time for a hot meal at home!

He took in the scene, the one he had played over in his mind so often in the last two years. As he walked down the lane, he tried to decide whether he would go to the front door or around to the kitchen door. He imagined the entire family now seated around the table for their dinner, so he decided to use the back door.

He went up the steps onto the back porch and rapped on the door with his knuckles. He heard a feminine voice ask who it was, and it was so great to hear Mother.

He realized he probably was alarming her as a stranger at her back door, so he called out, "It's me, Andrew."

The door was flung open, and there she stood in a wash dress covered with an apron. She was a picture of beauty, the mother of his children and the homemaker keeping the home fires burning and the farm running while he was off at war. For one of the few times in his life, Mother was speechless.

She embraced him tightly and whispered, "I can't believe you're home."

She took his hand and led him into the kitchen, where the children started screaming in delight. They ran to him and enveloped him in hugs. The youngest two, Alberta and Priscilla, hung on to his pant legs and squeezed. Albert came over and shook his father's hand.

Andrew took it all in and couldn't believe how much his offspring had grown. Andrew told everyone how happy he was to be home and that he would be there for almost a month. He said how much he was looking forward to Christmas as a family after so much time away. It seemed like forever until Mother could get the children reseated at the table and put a setting out for Father for his meal as well.

"Andrew, you must be starved," Mother said. "When was the last time you ate?"

"I can't remember the last time I sat at a proper dinner table," he answered. "But I did have a biscuit and coffee early this morning in Butler."

After a hearty meal, each of the family members took turns telling Father what had been happening while he was gone. He asked his children about school, how tall they were now, and what they had been doing for fun. Albert was anxious for Father to tour the barn and see the horses and livestock.

Andrew was pleased to see the good condition of both teams and excellent maintenance on all the equipment around the farm. He and Albert walked some of the rail fence lines and checked out the cattle. Albert was especially proud of a nice young Hereford bull calf he was raising. It was gentle and had filled out well on the corn and good hay they had put up over the summer.

At supper that night, Andrew surprised Mother and the family by saying, "In a couple days, your mother and I will be leaving for a trip to Butler. It will probably be an overnight trip. I have some business that will probably take most of the day in the city."

He didn't add that what he really wanted was to have a day or two alone with Mother after two years of being apart.

Albert volunteered that he could take care of things while they were gone. Over the next couple of days, Andrew spent time with each of the young children as well as with Albert, helping around the farm and with various projects. He and Albert took the wheels off the wagon, greased them, and reinstalled them back on the hubs.

Andrew hitched up the young team to the buggy early in the morning that Father and Mother were scheduled to depart for Butler. With more hugs all around, the parents said good-bye and climbed into the buggy, soon rolling down the road.

In Butler, they checked into the hotel on the square, and after putting their belongings in the room, they ventured down Main Street for some window shopping. Andrew had made special arrangements for a table for two at the hotel dining room. On the way back to the hotel, he stopped at a millinery shop and had Mother try on a new dress, hat, and fancy gloves.

She protested that it was far too much money, but he insisted that it was his gift to her as an early Christmas present. He insisted to the point that she acquiesced, and they had the clerk wrap up the new clothes so she could carry them back to the hotel. There, Andrew surprised her by telling her that he had made an appointment at a Chinese bathhouse next door and that they were going to be bathed separately and then she could change into her new clothing. He would put on fresh clothes as well. Mother had never been treated to such luxury, and Andrew told her he had been saving up for this surprise.

Freshly bathed and in new clothing, they returned to the hotel and enjoyed a fine steak dinner with apple pie for dessert. When finished, it was back to their room where they could enjoy time alone together without any children around.

Later, Andrew held Mother in his arms and told her how much he loved her and how much he had missed her. He expressed his sincere appreciation for everything she had done with the family and the farm while he did his duty to his country. As Mother gazed at the ceiling, she thought she had never been happier or more fortunate in her entire life than to have Andrew here tonight and to share this special day and evening with him.

The next morning, they traveled back to the farm in their buggy. For the next few days, Andrew spent each day with Albert examining and repairing the buggy, helping to harvest more firewood, stacking the wood in the woodshed, and working on fence repairs. There also were repairs needed around the house, with floorboards that had come loose and roof shingles needing to be secured.

Finally, it was two days before Christmas. At the noon meal, Andrew told all the children that they would have an adventure in the afternoon, as they were going out to cut a pine tree for their Christmas tree, bring it home, and decorate it. It had snowed a couple of times in the last week, so they took the sleigh and the young team and headed out around the big hill behind the farm where there was a stand of pine trees.

The family had great fun shaking the snow off some trees and examining them to make sure they picked the perfect pine to take home. With a few sharp blows from the axe, Andrew chopped it off at the base. They loaded it on the very back of the sleigh, and all the children climbed aboard, laughing and singing.

27

Holiday Festivities
on the Farm

Late in the afternoon of Christmas Eve, Andrew found two pieces of wood in his workroom and nailed them across each other to form a stand for the pine tree. He sawed off the bottom of the trunk and nailed through the stand into the tree. He carried it around to the front door of the house so they could position it in the living room. The younger children could not remember ever seeing a Christmas tree.

Andrew had several small candles, and he used a fine wire to wind each candle to the far end of a long branch. Next, he brought in a large pail of water just in case of an accidental fire. Meanwhile, Mother heated a large skillet filled with lard. As it melted and started splattering, she called all the children to the kitchen. When she was in Butler a few days ago, she had bought a pound of popcorn, something none of her children had ever seen.

They gathered around as she took off the lid over the skillet and poured the corn into the hot oil. Replacing the lid, she waited a few moments and then heard the first telltale pops and then an explosion of popping. She occasionally lifted the lid a bit, and white fluffy corn jumped out of the skillet. The children had looks of amazement at this transformation that was happening right before their eyes.

Soon, the popping sounds died down, and Mother poured the snow-white corn into a huge bowl, then sprinkled on salt.

"Now it's your turn to try some of this," Mother said. "This is a treat called popcorn."

The children squealed in delight as they experienced this new treat for the first time. While they all joined in, Mother heated another pot and popped more corn. This one she took to the room with the Christmas tree and brought out sewing needles with thread attached.

She pushed the needle through the first piece of popped corn, followed by another and another. Soon, all the children were busy stringing corn into garlands. Next, Mother showed them how to wrap the garlands on the tree. For the finale, she produced a small hand-sewn angel and placed it on the top of the tree.

In recent years, new songs for the Christmas season had become popular, including, "Jingle Bells," "We Three Kings," and "Up on the Rooftop." Mother had a beautiful voice and had learned the songs as part of the church choir. Father gathered everyone around the tree and told them he would like to say a prayer of thanks. Then Mother would sing carols, and finally he would light the candles and turn down the oil lamps.

Andrew explained that in the old country of Germany, the green tree symbolized the return of spring, while the candles had been added by the important church leader Martin Luther to celebrate the birth of Christ.

The children were in awe of the wonderful evening—Father home from the war, popcorn, and the wonderment of the candles glowing from the tree branches. Too soon, the festivities were over, and Father doused the flames on each candle to make certain they were extinguished. He announced that it was bedtime, and on Christmas morning, they would have an early breakfast, open gifts, and then all get dressed in their finest winter clothes and drive the sleigh to church services.

Mother arose early on Christmas morning and prepared a wonderful breakfast of pancakes, bacon, sausage, and fried potatoes. The tantalizing smells from the cooking awoke all the children, who quickly skipped across the cold floors upstairs and hurried down to the warmth of the kitchen and the big cookstove. After the hearty meal, Mother led them into the living room. The first gifts presented were the dolls Andrew had brought home, and the girls squealed in delight, each giving a name to their new proud possession. James and Samuel were also thrilled to receive their new jackknives, and Mother was surprised when Andrew presented her with the new thread and needles for sewing.

She went upstairs and slipped on her new dress and hat and came back down to show off the finery, parading around the room. Mother surprised Andrew with three pairs of new socks that she had knitted. For a soldier, new clean socks were a cherished gift.

Andrew and Albert headed to the barn where they harnessed the young team and hitched up the sleigh. Albert made sure all the robes were in place on the seats while Andrew attached sleigh bells to the harnesses.

The trip to church was beautiful as the wind had died down, and light snowfall added a magical cover to the landscape and trees. The area around the church was filling up with sleighs and buggies, and the sidewalk leading up the hill from Main Street to the church was full of parishioners climbing the hill for the services.

Once inside, Mother went back behind the pulpit and met with the other choir members, quickly going over the hymns they would sing today. A few moments later, the preacher, the Reverend Isaac Decker, took his place in the pulpit and began the services. He called out the names of members of the congregation who had been lost in the war or were missing. It was chilling to have him include John and Thomas Eshenbaugh, who were reported as taken prisoner of war in North Carolina and being held at Andersonville Prison in Georgia. Also mentioned was Phillip Eshenbaugh, who had been missing in action since the battles of the Wilderness last spring. Reverend Decker asked that the parishioners keep all of these men in their prayers. The hymns were beautiful, and then came a long sermon, followed by the collection of the offering, then the final blessing to end the service.

The last week of December was filled with Andrew working around the farm mending fences, chopping more firewood, and repairing the harnesses and equipment so it would be ready for the spring plowing and planting. New Year's Eve was celebrated with roast venison, potatoes, and canned peaches. Leave was just about over, and the trip back to war would begin in the morning, but Andrew wanted to enjoy the family gathered around the fireplace.

Mother made fresh popcorn, and she led the singing of Christmas songs and church hymns. Andrew closed his eyes and savored the beautiful sound of her voice. Toward midnight, the girls removed the decorations from the tree, and Andrew carried the tree out the back door and stuck it in a snowdrift. For the rest of the winter, Mother would put pieces of suet in the branches to feed the songbirds as the cold winter days continued.

Albert had begged to be permitted to celebrate the new year by firing the shotgun into the air, and Andrew consented. As midnight approached, Albert donned a heavy coat and took the single barrel .12-gauge gun out onto the back porch.

Andrew checked his pocket watch and gave Albert the countdown of five, four, three, two, one. The beginning of 1865 was heralded by the loud boom as Albert pointed the old shotgun skyward and pulled the trigger. He was surprised to hear a couple of other shots being fired, coming from the direction of West Sunbury.

28

Back to War

Early the next morning, breakfast was ready in the kitchen, and Andrew and Albert headed out to the barn to harness the young team to the sleigh. The plan was for Mother to accompany Albert and Andrew in the sleigh to the stagecoach station in Butler and then head back to the farm as soon as they said good-bye to Andrew. The weather was threatening more snow, and Mother wanted to get back to the farm before the roads became impassable.

They loaded up in the sleigh, covering up with robes and pulling their collars high around their ears. Andrew tossed his knapsack loaded with new socks, underwear, and homemade cookies into the back of the sleigh and called on the horses to move out. The young team trotted off full of energy into the cold morning air. Andrew held the reins, and the sleigh moved smoothly over the fresh snow. In less than three hours, they pulled up in front of the stagecoach station. William A. waved from the front doors and stepped out to give Mother a hand down from the sleigh. William A. said the stage would be on time and leaving in about an hour for Pittsburgh.

Mother and Albert warmed up in front of the big potbelly stove in the station house and quickly were ready to head back north to the farm ahead of the impending storm. Andrew walked her back to the sleigh and gave her a tight hug and kissed her good-bye. Albert stuck out his hand to shake his father's hand

and told him he wished him safe travels and a quick end to the war.

Mother took the reins and signaled for the team to move out. The snow had started to drift up in places, and that made it difficult to steer the sleigh through them. At one point, just a mile before getting home, she hit a snowdrift with the left front runner that lifted the sleigh high in the air. She slapped the horses hard with the reins to pull the sleigh back down. Albert flew in the air and grabbed the handrail on the sleigh to keep from being ejected.

She slowed the team and gave them a short break while she caught her breath and collected her robes. Then, uneventfully, they made the last mile to their lane and gratefully turned into the barn and exhaled a huge sigh of relief to be home safely.

At the stagecoach waiting area, Andrew and William A. warmed up by the big fire in the stove. When another passenger laid down a newspaper and left the station, Andrew picked it up and glanced at the latest news. He was startled to see an article about a ruling made last week where the local judge held a hearing for a man accused of robbery and attempted murder. The judge ruled that there was not enough evidence to hold the accused. The article detailed how the judge had explained that no one had come forth to identify Buckskin or say that in the fading daylight Buckskin had actually been a participant in the attempted robbery.

As he read further, it was clear that the accused was the same person who was dressed in buckskins and had been at the scene when William A. and Andrew had opened fire on the two robbers attempting to rob the coach a month earlier. William A. was appalled that both he and Andrew were named in the article as the Union soldiers who had shot the two robbers and wounded the buckskin-dressed character. The reporter also included their duty in the cavalry and even said Andrew was in the 14th Pennsylvania Cavalry and a potato farmer in West Sunbury. He handed the paper to Andrew to read. As Andrew read it, he felt the shock of seeing himself and William A. both named in the story and even their home location areas disclosed.

Andrew slowly lowered the newspaper and turned his face to William A. "Oh my," he said, "this puts our families at risk with this character freed from jail and us headed back to the war!"

Both men sat silently, thinking about the gravity of the situation. Just then, the stagecoach driver and the shotgun guard entered the room to greet the passengers and get them ready to load up. When they spotted Andrew and William A., the two rushed over to greet them and thank them again for their quick response a month ago to save their lives and take down the gunmen. They asked if Andrew and William A. were headed back to Pittsburgh. The driver said they had a light load today since it was a holiday and that he was going to seat Andrew and William A. inside the coach even though their tickets were only for seats up top in the open air.

Andrew expressed his gratitude for the seating but told the driver he was thinking about going back home considering the article in the paper and the release of the armed robber. The four men stood and discussed the situation. Finally, the driver said he did not want Andrew or William A. to be classified as deserters after all they had done for their service. He explained he would be back from Pittsburgh by tomorrow night, and he could organize the home guard to provide protection for their families.

Andrew and William A. had not shared with their wives and families any details of the shootings that occurred on their trip home a month ago. They decided they would ask the guard to provide the home guard service. Andrew also asked the driver to give them a few minutes, and he got paper and pen from the ticket agent and dashed off a letter to his wife explaining to her the details and tore out the article from the paper to mail to her as well. He wanted her to be aware of the situation and the potential threat from the man in buckskin.

The driver said he would mail the letter the next day when the post office reopened, but right now they needed to load up and head south to Pittsburgh. The coach was less than half filled, and the horses made good time to the halfway stop, the Dixon Inn. There, the driver and guard unhitched the team and met the stationmaster to bring out a new team while the passengers warmed up inside.

The driver shared with the stationmaster that the two heroes, William A. and Andrew, were part of the passenger list. They were given the hero's welcome they deserved with a hot meal and thanks all around.

Soon the coach and team were back on the road. Although snowflakes fell all the way into Pittsburgh, the roadway was passable, and the team arrived on schedule to the train station in Pittsburgh. William A. and Andrew made their way across to the train station and bought their tickets to Washington. The ticket agent told them it would be about two hours till boarding, so they walked to the restaurant at the end of the rotunda and ordered beef stew with freshly baked bread. They ate in silence, and when finished Andrew suggested they find their train and board early so they could get seats in the middle of the car away from the drafty doors.

On board an hour later, they both settled back and wrapped up in their greatcoats to ward off the cold night and await the departure. The car filled quickly, mostly with soldiers returning from leave. The mood was somber as the troops thought of their families and the month spent enjoying Christmas—and now their return to the war.

Eventually, the train jerked and slowly started gaining speed. Soon, they were chugging east through a cold, snowy moonlit night. Finally, William A. nudged Andrew and asked him if he'd figured out what to do about the buckskin robber who had been released by the judge. They both agreed this was a problem, as he now knew who they were and where they lived, with their families vulnerable.

Andrew concluded that there was nothing they could do to protect the families until they were home from the war, whenever that might be. Exhausted, they both fell asleep and only woke up when the train pulled into the station in Washington, D.C.

As they came off the train, a second lieutenant directed them to a line of tables where other officers held lists of train numbers, destinations, outfit locations, and departure times. When Andrew told the officer they were under General Sheridan's cavalry, he told them to run to track 5 and board, as the train was departing almost immediately. When they swung aboard, the train started moving, and they found they had to stand or sit in the passage-ways between adjoining cars.

Daylight was breaking as the train ground to a halt, and they could see the winter camp for the cavalry. Officers directed the troops as they stepped off the cars and sent them to their companies.

William A. shook hands with Andrew and said he had enjoyed his company as they traveled home and back, despite the adventures and mishaps, and hoped they would ride home together soon at the end of this terrible war.

Andrew found his company and then his bedroll, exactly as he'd left it a month ago. He reported to the officer of the day, who welcomed him back and told him there would be no duty until roll call tomorrow morning. He decided to check on chow and was able to grab coffee, sausage, and a biscuit. He then walked over to the 4th Pennsylvania Cavalry to find Will.

Will had been growing a beard for the past month, and it had come in full and jet black, so thick that Andrew did not recognize him at first. They were happy to see each other and shook hands, and Will grabbed two coffee cups and poured them each a cup. They took seats on logs in front of a fire. Andrew described Christmas on the farm and provided a detailed update on all the family members back home. He recalled how Mother was so pleased with the thread and needles and how happy the girls were to sit by the fireplace and admire the tree.

Finally, Andrew said, "We had a problem on the way home. Highwaymen tried to rob the stage halfway between Pittsburgh and Butler. Unfortunately for the robbers, between William A., oil workers, and me, two of them died at the scene, and a third one was wounded and captured."

Andrew went on to explain how the judge and court had decided to drop charges, and the buckskin-clad robber had been freed. When Andrew described him as dressed in buckskin, a tall rider with a crooked left arm, Will was shocked. He had never shared details of his encounter with the robber who had escaped when Blackie was shot, but quickly he realized that they had both encountered shooting episodes with the same bad man.

Andrew shared that the newspaper had identified him and William A. as two of the stagecoach shooters by name and where they lived. Will sat there to let this information sink in. Buckskin had already been within a mile of the farm when he tried to rob Mother and Will. Now he could check out potato farmers in the West Sunbury area and easily come looking for Father. With only young Albert there to protect her, Mother and the children were quite vulnerable. Andrew explained that the newspaper had also reported that he and William A. were in the army, so maybe Buckskin would wait till the war ended to come looking for them.

They had to part ways, as Will was on guard duty on a picket line that evening, and Andrew was anxious to get back to his outfit.

29

Sharpshooters

For Will, the rest of January was spent conducting patrols every day to watch for Confederate movements and potential raids. The Virginia weather offered little snow and mild temperatures that seldom fell below freezing. Troops spent much time cleaning their weapons and tack and grooming their horses.

In early February, Will received orders to join a formation of a hundred troopers. Each trooper was issued a medal with "Sharpshooter" inscribed on it over an image of a Sharps repeating rifle. They were told they were now a special detached squad and would report the following morning at six a.m., separate from the company. Members of this special detail should report to the quartermaster for new issue.

There, they were given new dark green uniforms and new Sharps rifles. On top of the rifle was a long brass scope. Both the scope and the rifle had been painted black to help conceal the snipers. The men gathered in small groups and chatted about this new turn of events. They marveled at the rifles they had been issued and how much the scopes magnified targets.

After mess the next morning, the hundred sharpshooters were broken into squads of ten men each and assigned a range master. They were taken to an open area that backed into a hillside and told they would learn to sight their new rifles and zoom in on targets by adjusting the scope. A fellow shooter would spot for each trooper and use a spotting scope to report the results of each round fired.

As the week progressed, the distance to the targets increased, and each sharpshooter was scored against his prior day's shooting and against all the other shooters' scores. At the end of each day, the scores were posted on a bulletin board.

For the second week, the troopers were taught how to conceal themselves in trees and underbrush, how to crawl flat on the ground to position themselves for stealth shots, and how to cover their muzzle immediately after firing to obscure any signs of gun smoke that might give away their position.

At the beginning of the third week, members of this special unit were assembled and told of their true mission. They were to be snipers, wreaking havoc on the encamped Confederates. These marksmen would primarily conceal themselves over-looking the enemy camps and carefully target officers, firing only if they had a clear shot. Then they would retreat after firing to avoid detection and capture. They were warned that the Confederates would likely execute any captured sharpshooters by firing squad.

Will was appalled at the role of sniper. He felt it was unsporting and made him an assassin. The sharpshooters had been separated from the general Union Army population and isolated during training, meals, and camping. The sharp-shooters talked among themselves over chow, and some were excited with their new assignment, convinced that their role would help hasten the end of the war. Others, like Will, hated the idea of being a sniper, taking down unsuspecting enemy soldiers unable to defend themselves. The sharpshooters also discussed that if they refused, they could be charged with dis-obeying orders and maybe even treason, a charge that could lead to one's execution by their own army.

That evening, they were called to order and told to report at three a.m. the following morning wearing their green sharpshooter uniform and armed with fifteen rounds of ammunition and their Sharps rifles. After a quick meal of biscuits and sausage, they mounted up. Each sharpshooter was accompanied by an outrider, who would help the shooter get secured in their shooting blind and then lead the shooter's horse away.

Will was ready with the black horse and rode off into the darkness to his assigned station five miles away, to a tall pine tree where he had a view three hundred yards from the encampment of General Lee's Confederate Army of Northern Virginia. Will had decided he did not want any horse hoofprints under his tree in case a Rebel patrol came by, so he dismounted some distance from his station and made his way in the dark to the base of his tree. Will climbed the branches through thick layers of needles until he was fifty feet above ground. He then found his seat on a large branch, where he could lean back against the truck of the tree.

Dawn was breaking as he watched his outrider ride off leading the black horse back toward the Union lines. Will wondered to himself how he had gotten in this position. If he followed orders and took out Confederate officers in their camp, Will felt this was akin to murder. He did not mind shooting anyone who was actively engaged in war, but he was highly conflicted with this sniping. If he were captured, he would surely be executed by a firing squad of Confederates after being found guilty of a war crime. If he refused to follow orders, he could be court-martialed by the Union Army, and the highest penalty was execution by his own army.

Dawn broke with a beautiful sunrise, and soon the rays were warming the air. Will could hear the Confederate troops being roused awake and horses neighing for feed. He could also smell the campfires being stirred to life to warm up the troops. Will used his field glasses to look over the activity. He was shocked at how gaunt and frail the troops appeared, many of them milling about barefoot. Many of them did not appear to have a coat but wrapped themselves in ragged blankets to fend off the cold.

Will scanned the entire campground and saw the cavalry horses grazing across the valley. They, too, appeared bony and lethargic. Will guessed there was no grain for the horses, only dead grass from last summer that the horses could feed on. Most of the horses had protruding hip bones and ribs showing, sure signs of slow starvation.

As Will sat in the branches of the pine tree, he thought about the rationale of the sniper program. Likely someone in the War Department in Washington had thought this one up and sent it to the field. Both sides had been using snipers during combat since the early days of the war but not to reign terror on encamped troops. He had heard that out west in Missouri, the Confederate raiders used snipers on both Union troops and civilians who were Yankee supporters.

Will pulled up his Sharps rifle and leveled it on the camp so he could use the scope to zero in on the activity there. He was glad for a calm morning, as he would not need to calculate wind speeds and the impact of it on any shot. He could see the tents clearly, and on a knoll above the encampments he saw five mounted riders. As they sat on their horses, they seemed to be awaiting something, and in a few minutes another rider rode up to the circle. The first riders made a semicircle to face the last one to arrive. Will could not see the men's insignia clearly enough to determine the rank of the riders, but he surmised that the rider facing the group was the ranking officer and the rest were awaiting orders.

He estimated the distance to be at five hundred yards, a long shot but not an impossible one. Will brought his rifle back to a rest position as he simply could not shoot another man in cold blood from ambush.

What to do? Following orders to shoot this way was not acceptable morally and religiously for Will. Not following orders was almost equally unacceptable. In his mind, the plan for sharpshooters was to create a reign of terror over the Confederates and to help them realize all was lost and it was time to surrender. A few more dead Confederate officers was not going to change the outcome of the war. It seemed all but over, and the surrender of General Lee would happen soon.

With determination, Will again raised his Sharps rifle. Through the scope, he could see the officers were still meeting. Will zeroed in on the horse of the top officer. He had a window for a chest shot or a head shot. Will hated the idea of shooting a horse, but to him it was a more acceptable idea than to shoot a defenseless officer.

Will had a dark towel he had suspended by a fine wire from the end of the barrel and a heavy glove around the receiver end of the rifle. Upon firing, he would quickly slide the towel over the end of the barrel to capture the smoke coming out of that end and slide the heavy glove over the trigger and shell chamber to mask smoke there.

Will again scoped out the riders, calculated the range, and set his range finder on the barrel to accommodate the fall rate of the shell. With little or no wind, he did not need to make further adjustments. He zeroed in on the officer's horse once again, exhaled, and pulled the trigger.

Sure to his shot, the horse went down instantly, and the officer was standing on the ground. The shooting had created a level of panic in the camp, and men everywhere were ducking for cover or grabbing their rifles. The remaining riders broke apart and scrambled away from the knoll to lower ground. Several troops on the ground pointed in different directions, seemingly to try to point out where they thought the shot had come from. Will anxiously watched to see if they were mounting a patrol to come search for him.

While all of this was ongoing, Will heard three separate shots from different directions. He quickly realized other sharpshooters had taken advantage of the confusion and had picked targets of the officers who had been mounted in the meeting. All three shots found their mark and tumbled Confederate riders from their saddles. Lee's army looked like a kicked-over anthill, with troops and horses scattering. Orders were being shouted seemingly from every direction. Soon, riders formed up to head out on patrol, while the shooters and riflemen dove to the trenches all around the perimeter. Medics rushed to the officers who had been shot off their mounts.

Will froze on his branch, knowing the consequences if he were detected. The other three shots had come from the north and east of the encampment, with Will on the west side. He watched as the patrols got their orders and breathed a huge sigh of relief as the patrols headed out to the north and east. Will also reckoned he would be holed up on his branch for the entire day as it would be too risky to descend to the ground. He had a rope inside his jacket and decided to tie himself to the tree trunk so he would not fall in case he fell asleep during the day.

The warm afternoon sun in late March made him sleepy, but he knew he had to remain alert. He strained as he thought he heard hoofbeats and then saw ten gray-clad cavalrymen ride up hard from behind him. But thankfully they were on the way back to the Confederate camp and rode past right under his tree.

When night fell, Will untied his rope, shouldered his rifle, and slowly made his way down the truck of the tree. He very quietly hit the ground, quickly got his bearings to the north, and headed toward Union Army lines five miles away. He knew there were pickets out in front of his army encampment, and he would need to bed down before he got too close to them and await daylight tomorrow. Moonlight gave him what light he needed to stay on the roadway, and he figured in an hour he had traveled at least three miles.

Time to bed down, Will decided, and he spotted a stand of pine trees and knew that under them would be a soft bed of needles and some shelter from the cold night air.

After a fitful night's sleep, Will made his way into camp and identified himself in the daylight to the Union sentry on picket duty and walked back into camp. He was glad to find the mess hall open, as he had not eaten in three days.

After a hearty meal, Will found his tent and slept a good ten hours to get rested. Late in the day, orders came down for all sharpshooters to assemble at five p.m. on the parade field. General Sheridan rode out and addressed all of them. First, he thanked them for their service and for risking their lives in the extraordinary exposure as sharpshooters. He then announced that one of the fellow shooters had been found by the Confederates, taken prisoner, and executed yesterday following the sniping on Lee's encampment. He asked for a moment of silence to pay tribute to their fallen comrade, a young man from Boston.

30

Back to Battle

With the sharpshooters still assembled before him, General Sheridan informed them their unit was being disbanded, and they were to return to their regularly assigned outfits the following morning. He said the public was outraged both in Richmond and in northern cities over their attack on the camp, and President Lincoln and Secretary of War Edwin Stanton had ordered them to stand down.

Two days later, March 25, 1865, General Lee launched a Confederate attack on Fort Stedman, near Petersburg. General Grant had been pressing Lee on all sides, trying to force a surrender, so Grant ordered a counterattack during the following week. Lee's army was severely weakened, short on food and ammunition, and facing massive desertions every day as troops felt the war's end was near. Grant hit Lee's forces hard at Five Forks, forcing Lee first to abandon Petersburg and then, on April 1, to abandon Richmond.

General Sheridan and the cavalry forces were the vanguard to ride into Richmond from the northwest, and General Sherman pushed in from the east and south. The Confederates set fire to the warehouse area of Richmond, burning cotton, food, and any supplies the Yankees could use. Winds swept the fires across the city, burning houses and buildings in the path, filling the air with smoke and ashes. As the Confederates abandoned Richmond, the Union Cavalry rode hard to contain them and keep Lee from either heading east to meet up with other Rebel forces or west to meet General Albert Johnson's Army of Tennessee.

Will's cavalry unit was in the vanguard, and nearby was Father's 14th Pennsylvania Cavalry and General Custer's Michigan Cavalry. Early on the morning of the second of April, Andrew's company was awakened and ordered to saddle up.

They headed into Richmond and rode to the capitol building that had just been abandoned the day before when Confederate President Jefferson Davis and his cabinet hastily abandoned the city and headed south, seeking somewhere they could set up new offices for the Confederacy.

When Union troops were called to order on the lawn of the Confederate capitol, they were informed that President Lincoln had taken a boat from Washington, D.C., and had just landed in Richmond. The 14th Pennsylvania Cavalry would provide him an escort and keep back the crowds. The President was already ashore and practically being mobbed by now-freed slaves who were crying and overwhelmed that President Lincoln had traveled to Richmond.

For two days, President Lincoln and his son Tad toured the city. One of the stops was at Libby Prison, the place that had held Union officers who had been captured. The facility was deplorable with overcrowding, little food, unsanitary conditions, and no windows to keep out the wind or rain. The prisoners had all been released just two days earlier, and Union doctors were treating many of them before they would be sent by rail to Washington, D.C., or Philadelphia army hospitals for further treatment.

Andrew found time to write to Mother, describing the feeling of euphoria the troops of the 14th felt, believing the war was almost over, and the pride they felt to be guarding President Lincoln. There was apprehension among the troops over their responsibility, and it seemed quite probable that a Confederate sympathizer could seize the chance to shoot the President of the hated Union. Still, the President traveled and walked among troops without evident fear. At midday of the third day of the President's visit, he returned to the *USS Malvern*, the riverboat that would take him back to Washington.

Once General Lee evacuated Richmond, he was desperate to escape General Grant, who was closing in on Lee from all sides. Lee first headed west, but General Sheridan and his cavalry turned him east. Next, he thought he could overrun the Union cavalry on the east and make it to the Carolinas, but Sheridan had more than nine thousand troops in the saddle, with Grant soon to arrive with his fifty thousand infantrymen and cannoneers. Lee turned toward Appomattox Court House, where a last-ditch effort was being made to resupply him by rail and a convoy of wagons laden with food and ammunition.

General Sheridan and the cavalry cut off the rail supply, and General Custer and the Michigan Cavalry captured the wagon train of supplies. When this news reached Lee, he knew the war was over. General Grant had sent peace envoys with white flag escorts for the past two days. Now it was Lee's turn to send his officers to Grant with a surrender letter.

31

At Appomattox Court House

At dawn on April 9, 1865, General Lee still thought he might escape to the east.

But after forced marches all night, Union troops, including the United States Colored Troops, had blocked Lee's escape. Lee sent out two letters to Grant, and the one received by Sheridan's cavalry was the first to Grant offering surrender by Lee.

The surrender was set to be held early afternoon at the home of Wilbur McLean. The Union cavalry was ordered to assemble in front of the house, and several infantry units were marched on the quickstep there as well. On the other side, Confederates did likewise, and both sides moved into formation. Orders were given to the Union troops to respect the Confederates and not gloat or taunt them.

Ironically, McLean's house in northern Virginia had been taken over by the Union Army early in the war and now his home where he had relocated much further south would be the setting to the surrender of General Lee and the Army of Northern Virginia.

Will felt exhausted, as he had been riding long days every day since the Confederates left Petersburg and had been on the forefront to meet Lee's army at each turn when they evacuated Richmond. He wheeled the black horse into a trot as the troops rode to the formation for the surrender. He leaned back in his saddle to admire the cloudless sky and beautiful spring day, knowing this day would forever be in his memory. By noon, troops on both sides had formed up in the fields of the McLean house and farm. Will turned in his saddle and spotted the regiment flag of the 14th Pennsylvania Cavalry and was pleased his father would also witness the surrender. Will knew William A.'s unit, the 4th Cavalry, would also be present. They would all celebrate together tonight.

Around one p.m., a cheer went up from the Confederate ranks as a group of horsemen rode up. At the head was General Robert E. Lee on his famous dapple gray horse, Traveler.

Dressed in a new gray uniform, General Lee moved with his usual confident and impressive bearing. He stopped in front of his troops and saluted them, which set off a round of cheers for the general. With that, he dismounted and entered the house, escorted by a half dozen officers.

An hour later, a roar went up from the Union side of the formation. Up rode General Ulysses S. Grant and his entourage of officers, including Generals Sherman, Sheridan, and Custer. In contrast to Lee's appearance, Grant's uniform and horse were splattered with mud and showed the road dust of the thirty or more miles he had ridden that morning. The officials rode to the front door and dismounted, turned to salute the troops, and then entered the house.

In less than an hour, all the officers emerged from the house. Grant saluted the Confederate troops and shook hands with Lee and rode off toward the Union camp. The Confederate soldiers dismounted and were read the terms of the surrender.

They were to line up and surrender all long guns, but they were permitted to keep sidearms. Southern men had gone to war with their own horses, so Grant permitted them to keep their mounts as well. Each soldier would be issued a pass for unimpeded travel, and the Union Army presses were already on hand printing them up. The troops were also informed that with the surrender of the Army of Northern Virginia, the Union Army would be providing twenty-five thousand meals that evening.

The Union soldiers were addressed and informed that this was only the surrender of one army of the south and other forces would still be hostile. In fact, the war would drag on for several weeks as some troops refused to give up and word of surrender was slow to reach troops as far west as Texas.

After the troops returned to camp and were dismissed, Will walked over to find Father. They sat and talked about what this all meant. Was the war over, or would they have more fighting to do? What would convince the remaining Rebels to surrender now that Lee had ended the war and the Confederate government was in flight? Both Andrew and Will were without answers to these questions that night, but both were elated that Lee had laid down arms.

❦

The nation was shocked and distraught six days later when President Abraham Lincoln was assassinated by John Wilkes Booth at Ford's Theatre in Washington, D.C. Grant and his troops were in mourning, and it was not understandable to them how this president could have led them to victory only to be shot from behind less than a week later.

William A., Andrew, and Will sat in shock and disbelief as the news spread on Saturday morning that President Lincoln had died from his gunshot wound. How could this be? He had just traveled to Richmond a few days earlier when cavalry had provided escort and protection after the city fell to Union troops.

Sadness spread across the encampment. The troops were exhausted after four years of war. They had only slightly settled down from their celebration of the surrender by General Robert E. Lee at Appomattox Court House. The assassination occurred on Good Friday, so Sunday was Easter. Will, Andrew, and William A. decided they would find a church for Easter service, but churches were packed wall to wall. Back at camp, the chaplain posted announcements that he would conduct both Easter and memorial services honoring President Lincoln.

Before dawn on Easter Sunday, the assembly field was filling up for ten a.m. services. By the time the chaplain mounted a platform, the entire area was crowded with soldiers standing shoulder to shoulder. Others had climbed nearby trees to hear the services.

The chaplain first honored Jesus and the resurrection with a traditional Easter morning sermon. The soldiers seemed restless, shifting their weight and swaying as they stood, awaiting the memorial for their slain president.

When the chaplain began his memorial speech, he could barely be heard. Choked up and with trembling voice, he recounted the shooting at Ford's Theatre in Washington, D.C., railing that a Southern assassin had killed the president and was on the loose. He prayed for the Union cavalrymen who were at the very moment serving as a detached unit seeking the killer and any accomplices.

The chaplain referenced how the newspapers were filled with stories and speculation about the assassin, the motive, and how this could have happened. As the service continued, grown men stood weeping—men who had seen comrades and enemies die on the battlefields. Many of these men had killed other men in close combat and now felt overcome with emotion that Lincoln had been shot dead just days after leading the nation through four years of war.

The chaplain spoke for more than two hours. By the end of his eulogy, there did not seem to be a dry eye on the grounds. Wailing could be heard in the far areas of the grounds, coming from a large gathering of now-free slaves who came to hear the service for Abraham Lincoln.

As the Sunday services wound down, soldiers could be seen all over the camp standing or sitting in small groups. Gone was the excitement over Lee's surrender, as the entire assemblage was hushed with a sorrowful pall hanging over the area. Many soldiers cried silently while others tried to compose letters to send home sharing their feelings of great loss, despair, and concern for what this meant for the war and the post-war peace period.

For twelve days, the troopers assigned to find the assassin scoured Maryland and the Virginia countryside. The escape path of John Wilkes Booth covered over ninety miles south into Virginia. The Sixteenth New York Cavalry was hot on his trail and received a tip that he might be at the farm of Richard Garrett. Garrett's son Jack grew suspicious of Booth and his traveling companion, David Herold, and told them to sleep in the barn, where he locked them in the tobacco barn. Around two a.m., the cavalry arrived and roughed up Richard Garrett, seeking information about the fugitives. Jack quickly told them the two men were locked in the tobacco barn. Immediately, the troopers and the detective with them surrounded the barn and demanded a surrender. Herold came out quickly, but Booth remained defiant and asked for a shoot-out. The barn was set afire to flush Booth out. Despite orders that he was to be taken alive, Sergeant Boston Corbett fired one bullet that struck Booth in the neck. Booth succumbed to his fatal shot on the front porch of the farmhouse.

For the balance of April, the cavalry units were sent out to Virginia cities and towns to establish law and order in the face of government collapse. The period of Reconstruction was started by Congress and new President Andrew Johnson, and martial law was established under military leadership.

At the end of April, most of the Federal troops were told that they would be moved to Washington, D.C., for a grand review in late May. Once in Washington, they were ordered to bathe, get shaves and haircuts, and exchange their old uniforms for new ones. The government did not want soldiers returning home filthy, disheveled, and wearing tattered clothes. Will imagined that he could be home by early June, and he gathered with William A. and Andrew that night to talk about plans for the future. As they talked around the campfire that night, many of the soldiers had found a supply of liquor so there was a lot of drinking, laughing, and occasionally fisticuffs.

Will felt overjoyed to talk about how they would get home, if they would be able to travel together, and what a homecoming would be like after so much time away. Will said he would like to go through Kittanning and visit the McNabbs on his way back to West Sunbury.

32

Headed West

Andrew listened to all the excitement from Will and William A. and then said, "Boys, I will not be joining you on the trip home. The War Department has informed the 14th Pennsylvania Cavalry that we signed up for three-year enlistments that began in November 1862, so we will not be discharged until November 1865 or about eight months after everyone else."

Andrew went on to tell them that the 14th would not be marching in the Grand Review but would report in two days for their future assignment.

"We have been told we are going west," he said. "Some think we are being shipped to Mexico to fight the French. Others think we are being sent to fight Indians on the Plains. We do not know, but we are upset since we signed up to fight in the war against the Confederates and that is over. Some men are talking of just leaving and walking home to Pennsylvania, but our commander said that is desertion and punishable by death by a firing squad."

That evening, Andrew, William A., and Will gathered at the campfire. Andrew was quite disappointed that he was being shipped somewhere else to fight in someone else's war and not home to his family at the end of the war with the South. He told the other two they needed to have a plan to deal with Buckskin, the highway robber they had all encountered and who had been preying on victims along the major roads north and south of

Butler. Andrew figured Buckskin would want revenge for the loss of his robber companions when they were shot by Andrew and William A.

Andrew also shared that they should get home quickly and for William A. to look for a job right away, as there would be many veterans returning to Butler also seeking work. As for Will, Andrew laid out a plan for what crops to plant this spring so that the farm would get back to full production.

Two days later, the 14th Pennsylvania Cavalry was ordered to the train station. All their gear and equipment had been loaded into freight cars and the horses into stock cars behind a set of engines. Soon, another train backed in beside the first one, and this one had a caboose, ten flatbed open cars, a coal car, and two engines. Each company was ordered to climb aboard a flatbed car, and a few of the younger troopers followed orders. They were quickly shouted at by veterans who told them to get off the train. A ride for over three hundred miles sitting or lying down on a hard flatbed open railcar was not something the veterans were willing to do. The troopers sat down on the ground and refused direct orders from their lieutenants and captains to climb onto the open railcars. Finally, the commander of the 14th, Colonel Schoonmaker, rode up to see what was causing the holdup. The captain reported that the men were refusing an order to load up on the cars. Schoonmaker told the men that they could be court-martialed, imprisoned, given a dishonorable discharge, and have future pension revoked. Dead silence followed his comments.

Finally, Andrew stood up. "Sir, I am a lowly private, Andrew H. Eshenbaugh, in Company M. I have been with you, as have most of these men, since November 1862. We have ridden thousands of miles, had over a hundred encounters with the Rebs, and lost several of our friends to death, capture, and disease. We have slept in the rain and in the snow, gone without rations, and followed every order given. Now you are taking us to an unknown destination, making us stay on long after the end of the war with the South. You order us to climb onto open railcars, where we have no seats, only to dangle our legs over the edge or lie down on the deck, be pelted by the smoke and cinders from the train engine, and ride at speed on a cold night. Some of us are likely to fall off the cars, none of us will be able to sleep, and all of us will be cold. We would just as soon be court-martialed and sent to jail as it does not sound any worse. I speak to you with no authority, but I am forty-one years old and speak to you as a man and as a senior trooper in years on this earth."

Colonel Schoonmaker was taken aback and stared at the men for a few minutes. Finally, he addressed the men.

"Private, I admire your courage to speak up for the men," the colonel said. "I understand the feelings you expressed. I will address this issue with my superiors. In the meanwhile, all troopers stand down and bed down as we are not leaving tonight."

At this news, a huge cheer erupted from the troops.

Early the next morning, the engine and flatbed cars pulled out, and in their place, ten passenger cars were backed into the siding. Each company loaded into a car, and the freight train next to them also fired up. Shortly before nine a.m., the trains carrying the 14th Cavalry pulled out of Washington, D.C., headed west, destination unknown to the thousand troopers onboard.

The ride through the Cumberland Gap and the tunnels of the Baltimore and Ohio Railroad were familiar, and the troopers were elated to see the hills of Pennsylvania once again. There were a couple of stops for more firewood and water for the boilers, and then after about ten hours the train pulled into Pittsburgh.

Before the train stopped, officers addressed the men in each car and warned them that if they got off the train and deserted, they could be hunted down, court-martialed, and possibly even executed. At the least, they would be disbarred from a future pension. They were told they had an hour in the station to use the facilities, stretch their legs, and be back on board. Despite all the warnings, about a hundred troopers left the train and headed home.

While armed soldiers tried to round up the deserters, the whistle blew, roll call was taken, and notes were made of those who went AWOL. Soon, the engine built up steam and rolled out, with the troops on board seeing the Ohio River along the tracks. An hour after departure, a captain addressed each company.

"Men, we are headed to Cincinnati, Ohio. From there, we will transfer to riverboats to St. Louis, and then upriver to Fort Leavenworth, Kansas, where we will be stationed. It will take about ten days total, and when you are in St. Louis, you may want to stock up on any personal items as the PX at Fort Leavenworth is only lightly stocked."

The scenery along the Ohio River was much like Pennsylvania with flat river bottom land and rolling hills. To the south side, there were mountains in the distance, and most troopers slept in the warm cars with springtime sunlight filling the windows. The men were excited to exit the train in Cincinnati and march to the river docks. Most of them had never seen a riverboat, and they were now assembled beside several stern-wheelers and a few side-wheelers. The horses and gear were loaded on open barges behind the side-wheel boats, and finally the orders came for the troopers to board the stern-wheel boats.

Three hundred troopers were loaded onto each boat. With much whistle-blowing and shouting of orders, lines were cast free, and each boat maneuvered away from the dock and out into the Ohio River, headed for St. Louis. Late on the second day, the skyline of St. Louis appeared on the port side of the boats, and before dark they had pulled up to the docks and tied up.

Orders came down that all men would have a forty-eight-hour shore leave, and they would depart at four p.m. two days later. Some of the younger troopers headed immediately for the bars and brothels along the wharf. Andrew and his pals found a hotel with a good dining room and decided to enjoy a steak dinner and a couple of whiskeys afterward, suspecting that the food and whiskey where they were headed in Kansas would not be high quality.

Curious about this city, Andrew had heard a lot of people had come here from Germany. He felt comfortable mingling and enjoying German foods and pastries in the shops. He was fascinated at the amount of construction and masonry work building new structures out of block and brick. Several new breweries were also under construction, and one barkeep told him that the surrounding farmlands, as well as river transportation, brought them big supplies of wheat, oats, barley, and all they needed to brew and ship beer.

Two days later, the troops loaded up again, this time with new crews on the riverboats as they headed up the Mississippi River. Standing on the upper deck, Andrew gazed out across the river, which he estimated to be at least a mile wide. Its current was swift, made so by spring rains, but now they were going upstream against the flow. The steam engines whirled and puffed to turn the paddlewheels against the current, and progress was slow but steady.

It took about four days to reach a fork in the river, and they steamed left into a muddy, brown river. They were told they were now on the Missouri River, which carried soil from the spring runoff all the way from the base of the Rocky Mountains, far to the west.

The land on both sides of the river was above bluffs but then stretched away flat as far as the eye could see. Andrew could only dream of what it would be like to farm here, on flat, fertile fields as compared to the rocky hillside he called home in Butler County, Pennsylvania.

Finally, two days later, they pulled up to a wharf sticking out in the river and tied up. Each boat took turns unloading and moving away from the one dock. Once ashore, the troopers were ordered to unload the supply boats and help the horses onto land. Supply wagons were loaded, and the caravan of troopers and wagons moved away from the river.

Eventually, Fort Leavenworth came in view. It was all made of wooden posts in a huge square and a main gate leading into the compound. Troopers were assigned barracks by company, and horses were picketed in the center court, where they were fed and watered. Each company was welcomed to the fort with their first hot meal in days, and then the men bedded down for the night.

Soon, they settled into a routine of mounted patrols going out from the fort each morning. They were told they were to scout for Indians, although they never saw any. Other days, they escorted wagon trains headed west, many of them with former Union soldiers seeking their fortunes out west.

33

Mustering Out

Will thought about his father, so many miles away and still serving in the army despite believing his enlistment duties had been fulfilled. When the 14th Pennsylvania Cavalry pulled out of Washington, D.C., neither the troops on board nor those left behind knew where the 14th was headed. Were they going to Mexico to fight against the French? No one knew.

Will offered up a prayer for his father's safety even as he stretched out in his tent on the meadow in front of the White House. All around him, he heard the chatter and celebrations from the hundred thousand Federal troops who were here for the Grand Review, a parade of the armies that served the North in the fight along the eastern front.

Many of the men were having a grand time of it, spending their money on drink and women. Will was determined to remain sober and level-headed, as he was fully focused on heading home now that the fighting was over. His next thoughts wandered to the hills of home and family. The month of May was winding down, and he thought ahead to the days in the coming summer when he and Albert would make hay, harvest the grain and corn that Albert was busy planting, and repair buildings for the winter ahead.

Orders came down to be mounted the following morning in full uniform and be ready to move out by eight a.m. Dawn brought a beautiful May morning, and the mounted cavalry units went on parade first, followed by Union infantry veterans. The sidewalks for miles were packed with civilians who had come from all over to honor the soldiers.

Will felt great pride to see so many people turn out to pay tribute to them. The black horse tossed his head and acted like the parade was being held in his honor. Children waved and young women threw flowers or waved their hankies at the parade.

The parade stretched six miles long and took five hours to pass a point. They rode past the White House and Will bowed his head to pay honor to Abraham Lincoln, tragically assassinated just a few weeks before.

A few days later, Will stepped down from the train he had ridden to Pittsburgh. He looked around at the station where he had departed early last winter, marveling at how much had happened in the months since he passed through here on his way to the war.

After the troops gathered their belongings, they fell into formation. They lined up before the quartermaster offices to square up with the government. They could buy their pistol for two dollars, a rifle for five dollars, or a saddle horse for five dollars as well. Some chose just to take their last pay of twelve dollars, others took a horse, their pistol, and a Sharps rifle and squared up.

For some reason, the government had never charged Will for his special Sharps rifle with the sniper scope, so he was ready for his discharge. Fortunately, the quartermaster owed him for use of the black horse, so Will was cashiered out with his pay and twenty-five dollars for the army's use of the horse. He walked back to his outfit with thirty-five dollars in his pocket after buying his Colt .44 for two dollars.

Back in formation, Will spotted William A. walking by. They chatted a bit about how good it was to be back close to home. William A. said he was going to head to the train station and buy a ticket to Butler as soon as they were discharged. Will planned to ride up along the Allegheny River to Kittanning to see the McNabb family for a couple of days and then head to the farm in West Sunbury with plans to be there by the end of May.

William A. said he hoped to find work in the iron and steel plant in Butler. Will said he was going to help Albert on the farm for the summer and maybe head to the oil fields in the fall after all the farm work was done. Will said he had seen so many men headed there last November and felt like there could be good jobs to be had.

Finally, the troops were called to attention, and Colonel Schoonmaker rode up to address them. He thanked them for their service and wished them all well. He said he planned to take a position in management at the Erie-Lackawanna Railroad, and if anyone was looking for work, they should come by their offices near the train station. With that, they were told to line up with their company clerk and receive their discharge papers. In less than a half hour, Will had his signed papers and was freed from his army duties.

Will headed back to the stock cars, where the horses had been loaded. They had been separated into pens for privately owned stock and government-owned mounts. Will quickly signed for his black horse, swung by the equipment car, and picked up his saddle and tack.

Will led his horse out of the railyard and down to the river for a drink. Across the street was a hotel that offered meals, and Will tied the horse in front. Inside the hotel, he saw a dining counter where he found a seat. He ordered a plate of beef and mashed potatoes, asking the waiter to add two sausage biscuit sandwiches to the order.

Will decided to eat big for his fifty-mile ride to Kittanning. When finished, he packed the two biscuits into his bag, paid the waiter, and picked up the reins of the black horse at the hitching rail. Next door was a livery stable, and a stop there was in order. Will purchased a nose bag of oats and a five-pound bag of oats to tie to his saddle.

Once the black horse had finished eating, Will led him to the water trough for a deep drink. Will tied the haversack to the back of the saddle and slung the oats across the front if it, strapped the Sharps rifle to the right side and his bedroll behind the cantle.

34

Up the River

Satisfied that he was ready to ride, Will climbed aboard the black horse and pointed him north along the east bank of the Allegheny River. It was about two p.m., and Will figured he could cover maybe fifteen miles by dark. He planned to sleep just off the road in the woods unless he spied a better option. He figured a hard ride tomorrow would cover the remaining thirty-five miles, and he would surprise the McNabbs tomorrow evening before dark if the ride went well.

The road along the river had dried up after all the mud from the spring rains, and the horse was well rested and raring to go. Will was surprised at how many veterans he passed walking north along the river. Close to dark, he came upon an encampment along the river. It was made up of Union soldiers, who waved him over and offered him a place to spend the night. Will hesitated a moment, and a grizzled ex-sergeant warned him that highwaymen were busy bushwhacking soldiers traveling alone and robbing them of their pay and weapons. Those with horses were even better targets, he said, as they likely had a rifle and maybe a revolver, so they were good pickings for a robber.

Will found a grassy area where he picketed the black horse, fed it a ration of oats, and spread out his banket under a pine tree for a soft bed of pine needles under him and branches to cover him from the dew. After wolfing down a sausage biscuit, Will stretched out under the stars. He realized that with an early start tomorrow, he might make it to Kittanning by mid-afternoon and surprise the McNabb family. They were now part of the Minteer household after Mrs. McNabb married Mr. John Minteer, Harry's uncle, following the death of her husband. Exhausted after a hard day's ride, Will fell asleep in minutes.

⸎

The soft neighing of the black horse awoke Will well before dawn. Quietly, he filled a quart of oats in the nose bag and fed his mount. While the horse ate, Will dug a biscuit out of his haversack and choked down a cold breakfast. The black horse was again well rested and struck a quick trot headed north. The day warmed into another glorious spring day with trees in full bloom and flowers everywhere. Will loved seeing the newborn calves, lambs, and colts frolicking in the sun or stretched out in full-blown naps in the pastures along the road.

The miles clicked off as they made great time and passed many veterans trudging north as well. Everyone was in a good mood as they were headed home from the war. Will stopped mid-morning along the river to rest his horse and let it have its fill of water. He struck up a conversation with three men in civilian clothes. Will commented that it was good to see folks without uniforms, and one of them mentioned that he had been home for over a week and was now headed to the oil fields around Oil City, about fifty miles north. Will said he had seen a lot of men going that direction last fall and was thinking that maybe he would head there at the end of the summer. But first he wanted to see his family and help his brother on the farm till the harvests were done.

Without delay, Will mounted up and headed back up the river. In an hour, he found himself along a stretch of the river that seemed isolated, and soon he spotted two figures standing in the shadows of a turn in the road. For some reason, they seemed suspicious, so Will eased his big Colt .44 out of the holster and held it across his saddle hidden by the pommel. As he approached them, one of them stepped out a bit and held up his hand. Will slowed and halted about ten yards from the man. He was holding a single-shot Enfield rifle across his torso. Will could see it was not cocked. A quick glance at the companion showed he was a younger and slightly built youth who was not displaying any arms other than a big knife still in its sheath.

"Get off the horse and gimme your money now!" screamed the filthy highwayman.

Will quickly leveled the big .44 and shot him in the thigh. Down went the robber, screaming in pain. His companion ran for the woods, and Will dismounted, seized the rifle from the scoundrel, and quickly tied his hands using the robber's suspenders.

"You have no idea how lucky you are today," Will sneered. "The last man who tried to rob me I shot and killed on the road, and I am riding his horse. I am going to leave you here and hopefully you do not bleed to death before someone comes along, or your cowardly friend returns to help you."

Will remounted and whirled the black horse back onto the road north. He was glad he did not need to take the man's life. He'd had enough of killing in the last eight months to last a lifetime or more.

Will put the black horse into a lope and put as much distance between the robber and himself as he quickly could. The horse was up to the task and kept up the lope for an hour or more. Around noon, Will slowed him to a walk to rest him and realized they would soon be into Kittanning. As he entered town, great memories returned of the time spent here last winter. Soon, he turned down the street to the McNabb house and tied up the black horse in front of the house. He was apprehensive, not sure if they still lived here or had moved to the Minteer house.

As he knocked on the front door, a woman called out asking who was there. Will quickly identified himself and said he was looking for the McNabb-Minteer family. She shouted back that they lived four houses up the street on the right. Will thanked her and led his horse to the Minteer house. Little Bill answered the door, and right behind him came Sara and Laura. Sara about knocked Bill over to open the door and rush to hug Will. In her five-year-old exuberance, she jumped into Will's arms.

35

Happiness in Kittanning

Right behind the children, Mrs. Minteer came striding toward the door. She blinked and could not believe her eyes. It took a moment to see that this young man was Will, the soldier who had matured at war and grown a full black beard. Plus, he was tanned and weather-beaten from the wind, rain, and sun since he left here last winter.

"Oh my stars, Will, I am so happy to see you safely home!" she called out. "My, how you have grown into a handsome young man. Come in. You must be famished for a home-cooked meal, and I have a big roast of beef simmering for supper tonight. Mr. Minteer will be home from work in an hour. He now runs the sawmill where you worked, and they are busy six days a week, as demand for lumber is sky-high since the war is over. Oh my, how I gush on—you have not said a word or even had the chance to."

They stepped into the parlor, and the youngsters circled around while Mrs. Minteer fetched a pitcher of cold spring water and glasses. Will spent the next hour filling them in on his travels, the surrender of General Lee and the Grand Review in Washington, and then the train ride home. Finally, he said he had neglected to water the black horse, unsaddle him, and give him his grain, but he would be right back.

When he came back in, Sara was the first to greet him again with a big hug.

"I have a question for you," she said. "Why does your horse not have a name? You always just say 'black horse,' but did you ever name him?"

Amused at her curiosity, Will wondered to himself why he had never named him. "Sara, I would be honored if you would pick a name for my horse."

"Of course," she said. "I would call him Scout, after the dog you told me you had."

"Perfect," laughed Will. "He will be Scout from now on."

When Mr. Minteer came home from work and washed up on the back porch, they all sat around the kitchen table. Mr. Minteer wanted to know all about Will's time in the cavalry and asked about Andrew and how he was doing. They had known each other for years through the late Bill McNabb.

After supper, Will and the three youngsters held hands and walked to the river to watch the sunset. Sara said she just loved having Will visit and felt so happy he had come home from the war. A tear ran down her cheek as she said she wished her father could come home too.

Back at the house, Will waited as Mrs. Minteer tucked the three youngsters in for the night. When she came back downstairs, he told her how much he appreciated the time spent with her and the family. He said he was happy that she had found love and marriage with Mr. Minteer and a good home for Laura, Sara, and Billy.

He said as much as he enjoyed visiting, he felt eager to move down the road and head home to his family in West Sunbury. He said he'd be riding out early in the morning. Mrs. Minteer said she'd be glad to make him a nice breakfast and pack him sausage biscuits for the road.

Will saddled Scout before dawn and gobbled down the big breakfast of bacon and eggs, along with fresh bread and hot coffee. He said good-bye to Mr. Minteer and hugged Mrs.

Minteer, asking her to hug each of the children when they got up later. With that, he went out to the hitching rail and stepped onto Scout, pointing him west. He found the road that ran through the valleys to Butler and started out on the ride of thirty-five miles.

36

Homeward

As he rode, Will planned for his time in Butler. He'd have to sleep along the road that night and then ride into town the next afternoon. He decided his first stop would be the sheriff's office. As he rode up to Main Street, the city was bustling and many soldiers still in uniform were headed home from the war. Will knew the sheriff had his office at the top of the hill next to the courthouse, so he rode up and tied off Scout.

When he entered and asked to see the sheriff, the deputy did not seem willing to interrupt the sheriff, but Will persisted.

"I am just now returning from war," he announced. "It was my father and my uncle who saved the stagecoach from being robbed back in December."

The sheriff, who heard the conversation, immediately warmed up. "Oh, I am glad to meet you and grateful for your kinfolk. Brave men. Honestly, I couldn't understand how the court could release that robber. I respect the court but don't always agree with it."

Will asked the sheriff if he'd seen the robber since then.

"No, I haven't, thank goodness," the sheriff answered. "I've not seen him since the release, but lately, lone soldiers walking home from the war have been robbed by a gunman on a light-colored horse. Some said the robber was wearing a Union Army jacket with the stripes of a sergeant on the sleeves and buckskin breeches. But who knows? There are lots of thieves on the highways these days."

Will thanked the sheriff and rode up Main Street to the general store where he had sold potatoes last fall. At first, Mr. McCarrier did not recognize Will with his uniform and black beard but then shook his hand firmly to welcome him home. He asked about Andrew, and Will gave him the story of the 14th Pennsylvania Cavalry being sent out west somewhere until November. Mr. McCarrier said he could not believe the army wouldn't send home men who had been fighting for over two years.

Almost as an afterthought, Mr. McCarrier said, "By the way, a man was in here asking about you. Said he might want to buy potatoes from you this fall if you were growing any. He wanted to know your name and where you might be found. He seemed a bit suspicious, so I told him I did not recall anything about you or where you hailed from."

Will asked for a description and was alarmed that it matched what the sheriff said—a man wearing a Union Army jacket, buckskin breeches, and a kepi hat was asking around town about Will and the potato farm.

Down the street, the lights were lit in Kelly's Tavern, so Will decided to stop in and say hello to Mr. Kelly. There he was, behind the bar, wearing a white apron. He greeted Will with a friendly, "Howdy, soldier, will it be beer or whiskey?"

"Doubt you'd be offering me drink if you recognized me," Will replied. "I'm Will Eshenbaugh, Andrew's son. How were the potatoes that you bought from me?"

Kelly was shocked, as he had not recognized the man in front of him. Will had muscled up even more and now had a full black beard as well.

After they exchanged greetings, Will caught Kelly up on the war news and the story of Andrew being shipped off to finish out another six months of his enlistment. Kelly then shared a story of his own.

"Will, a fellow was in here a few days ago looking for information about a farmer," Kelly explained. "He said he heard the best potatoes around came from a farm out toward West Sunbury and that he was in the market to buy a supply of potatoes for the oil fields. I wanted to help your family in these hard times, so I told him he might want to ride out to the farm. I mentioned that you and your father were off at war, so there may not be potatoes to be had. But he could go and see. I told him to look for the Eshenbaugh farm about a mile north of the railroad crossing at Mahood and a mile south of town. Will, I hope he was able to find the farm and maybe your brother was able to sell him some potatoes."

Will drew a deep breath when Kelly described the man as dressed in an army jacket and buckskin pants and having a deformed left arm.

Oh no! Will thought immediately. *Buckskin now knows our name and might put together that I am related to one of the Eshenbaughs who shot him and killed his two bushwhacker companions.*

Will also speculated that Buckskin had figured out who he was and that he had shot his partner near the railroad crossing at Mahood, and then his father and uncle had shot his two scoundrel partners from atop the stagecoach.

Will decided he would have to deal with Buckskin directly and soon if he expected any peace now that he was home. He went back to the sheriff's office to see if there was a pattern to the robberies. As they discussed dates and times, the sheriff realized that the crimes occurred shortly after the *Butler Eagle* would carry a story about another outfit returning from the war by train or stagecoach. Apparently, the robber then figured out from the article where the returning troops lived and preyed on them on the secondary roads back home where they would be more isolated.   Sure enough, the *Butler Eagle* carried a report that the Fifty-Ninth Pennsylvania Infantry had arrived in Pittsburgh and had been discharged. The report also said most of the men were from Butler County and many from the West Sunbury area. Will figured this was it—the targets Buckskin was looking for with a lot of men walking north on the roads to and from Butler. Will decided to settle in on a hillside overlooking a spring-fed water trough about three miles north of Butler. He hid Scout in some underbrush and found a broad maple tree where he could set up a perch and have a clear view of the road below him. He hauled up his Sharps sniper rifle with the scope along with a pair of field glasses.

A steady flow of soldiers walked north, but most were in groups of three or four. Finally, a lone trooper came into view and stopped to drink and rest. He took a seat on a large rock near the water hole and rested a Sharps rifle across his thighs. Just then, a rider on a light-colored horse came out of the woods and rode toward the lone trooper.

The rider was wearing a blue Union Army jacket, a kepi hat, and buckskin trousers. Will was sure this was his Buckskin nemesis, and Will leveled his Sharps rifle on the chest of the rider, awaiting what was next. Will knew if he shot the rider unprovoked that he might be charged with murder, so any shooting needed to be self-defense or in the aid of someone in danger.

As Will watched, the seated soldier simply leveled his rifle on the rider. While Will could not hear the dialogue, it was only moments until the rider wheeled his horse away and rode north up the highway. *Well,* thought Will, *that was my man for sure, and he is riding toward West Sunbury and my home, so I'm sure we will meet again and probably soon.*

Darkness was falling, and Will felt exhausted. He found a spot off the road and under a copse of pines, where he could spread his ground cloth and bedroll. He would guide Scout to nearby grass to graze and then try to get a good night's sleep. Tomorrow would be a big day, as he was only a couple of hours' ride to home and the farm.

Before the sun broke above the eastern horizon, Scout whinnied softly and made his low rumbling sound indicating he wanted to be fed. Will fed Scout the last quart of oats and finished the last biscuit and sausage left in his saddlebag.

Perfect timing, Will thought. *We are out of food and grain, but before noon we will be home on the farm.*

As he rode north along the familiar road between Butler and West Sunbury, Will kept a sharp eye out for the buckskin rider, fearful the highwayman may target Will as a potential victim to rob or, worse yet, realize who he was and shoot him on sight.

Close to home, Will came upon the spot where Buckskin and his accomplice had tried to rob him and Mother last fall. Will crossed the railroad tracks and proceeded over the small bridge across Muddy Creek. In another mile, he cleared out of the woods and saw the valley ahead. The family farm straddled the road. Most of the cultivated fields and all the buildings and house were on the west side of the road.

On the east side rose a steep hill, which some said was the highest elevation in the county, with most of it still covered in virgin forest of huge oak and maple trees. What portions had been cleared by Andrew and his father years ago were bordered with split-rail fences and used as pasture for a few head of cattle.

Will slowed Scout and let the view sink in. This was what he thought about almost every night, imagining what his return home would be like. He was sure Mother knew his outfit would be home any day now and the *Butler Eagle* had been busy tracking returning Federal units.

Up the valley, Will could see Albert with a team pulling a one-row corn planter, and it looked like he had been busy since dawn planting. He figured Albert would be thrilled to see him, especially since it meant an extra pair of hands for the farm work. Smoke rose from the chimney above the kitchen in the two-story wood-frame house. That probably meant Mother was cooking on the woodstove, and Will suddenly felt hungry at the mere thought of eating her home cooking.

Will nudged Scout into a trot up the road to the farm lane and turned down the lane to the house. As he approached the front porch, he saw Albert stop at the end of the corn row and gaze toward him. Immediately, Albert let out a shout, tied off the team, and started running across the fields toward the house. That apparently got Mother's attention, as the front door opened, and she stepped out on the porch to see what was causing all the commotion. Behind her came Annis, Alberta, Isabella, and Priscilla, the little sisters trailing close behind Mother. James and Samuel were not far behind, curious about all the excitement in the yard.

Will slid off Scout and gathered Mother in his arms with his little sisters hanging onto his pant legs. Albert burst around the corner of the house on a dead run and joined in the celebration as they all danced around Will and Mother. Finally, Mother suggested they all go inside, and she would serve freshly baked rolls and a batch of sugar cookies, a rarity in the hard times of wartime lack of supplies.

They hadn't taken more than a dozen steps along the south side of the house when the first rifle shot cracked like lightning overhead.

Crack!

Will jerked as if punched, staggering back against Scout. Pain lit up his left shoulder like fire. He gritted his teeth, reached for the Sharps rifle in the scabbard just as—

Crack!

The second shot ripped through the air. Behind him, Mother screamed.

"Mama!" one of the girls cried.

Will spun in time to see her stumble, clutching her left side. Blood seeped through her dress. She collapsed into Albert's arms, gasping, a crimson stain already spreading across her bodice.

Will's voice came out hoarse, furious. "Albert, get them inside! Take Mother and the girls down to the cellar. Lock the door behind you!"

Albert nodded, lifting Mother carefully as the girls crowded around in a panic.

"I've got her, I've got her!" he said, half carrying, half dragging her through the back kitchen door.

Will turned, the pain in his shoulder nearly bringing him to his knees. But he shook it off. *Not now.*

The shooter had to be up on the east ridge—the high ground. Smart. Deadly.

Will slipped around the back of the house, hugging the shadows, Sharps rifle cradled in his good arm. Blood dripped down his sleeve, but he forced himself forward until he reached the thick shrubbery at the north end. He dropped low and raised the rifle, flipping open the scope with trembling fingers.

The hillside loomed across from him, cloaked in brush and towering trees. Perfect cover.

Come on. Show yourself.

He scanned for movement. Leaves. Branches. Nothing. Then—there—a flash of tan. A horse. Light-colored, nearly golden in the fading light.

Will narrowed his eyes.

It was Buckskin's horse.

Slowly, carefully, Will traced along the animal's side until he caught sight of a figure—mostly obscured, standing behind the horse's forelegs. Blending in with the horse's color. A trick. Clever.

But not clever enough.

The man was bareheaded now, his kepi gone. A Sharps rifle rested across the saddle, ready for another shot. Will's breath caught. He steadied the scope and found the man's face—just the upper half of it—peeking above the saddle.

It *was* Buckskin.

One shot, Will thought. *You get one shot.*

His training surged to the surface. Wind: still. Distance: uphill—advantageous. He adjusted for height, placed the crosshairs square between Buckskin's eyes. The scope bounced with his heartbeat.

He took a breath. Held it. The world went still.

Exhale . . . squeeze . . .

Boom!

The Sharps rifle roared. A red mist exploded from Buckskin's head. The man dropped without a sound, legs folding beneath him like cloth. The pale horse screamed and bolted, crashing up over the ridge and vanishing into the trees.

Will kept the scope steady for a beat longer. No movement. No more shots. Just Buckskin's lifeless body crumpled right where he had stood.

The threat was gone.

Suddenly dizzy, Will lowered the rifle and stood up too fast. Pain lashed across his shoulder, and he staggered, catching himself against the porch railing. Blood soaked through his jacket and ran down his arm.

He stumbled toward the kitchen, calling out hoarsely, "Albert! It's done. He's gone. Bring them up—now!"

Down in the basement, Albert held a lantern aloft. Its flickering light caught Mother lying on a stack of burlap bags, pale and bleeding. Her eyes fluttered open as Will knelt beside her.

"Will," she whispered. "You're hurt."

"So are you, Mama." He took her hand. It felt limp and far too cold.

"Can you walk?"

"I—I'll try . . ."

Albert moved quickly, slipping an arm under her shoulders and lifting her gently. Together they helped her up the stairs.

Will followed, his own legs heavy. He had seen enough wounded men in the past six months to know the signs—shock, bleeding, infection. Time was critical.

"We've got to clean these wounds," he muttered, thinking out loud. "Alcohol. Mama, do we have any?"

She hesitated. "There's a bottle . . . in the nightstand. Andrew brought it home at Christmas. I wouldn't let him open it."

Will nodded. "We need it now."

Albert dashed off, returning seconds later with the bottle of whiskey. Will uncorked it and handed it over.

"This is going to sting, Mama," Albert warned.

"I know. Do it."

Albert cleaned her wound first, dabbing away blood with a clean cotton cloth, then poured the whiskey into the open gash. She gasped, arching in pain, but never cried out.

Will watched her closely, fear tightening in his chest. Then Albert turned to him.

"Your turn."

Will stripped off his jacket, then his shirt. The long underwear was soaked with blood. Albert cut it away, revealing the wound. A clean pass—flesh only.

"Straight through," Albert said. "No bone."

Will winced as the whiskey hit raw tissue. "Feels like hell anyway."

Albert dressed and bound the wound as best he could, tying it off with strips of cloth.

Will slumped into a chair, breathing hard.

Outside, the night was still. The rifleman in buckskin was gone. But the cost of that quiet had bled into the floorboards of the house.

He looked toward his mother and whispered, "We're alive. That's what matters."

37

Get the Doctor!

Will pulled Albert close to him so no one would hear. "Albert, take my horse and ride to town. Go to the store and find Mr. Breadon or Dr. McCarrier. Tell them both Mother and I have been shot from ambush by the buckskin highwayman. Ask him if Dr. McCarrier can come quickly to the farm. I know he is mostly a dentist, but there is no one else in town. Also ask them to wire the sheriff in Butler to come out since the robber has been shot and killed. Also ask if they can have Mr. Young, the undertaker, come out to pick up the body of the dead shooter."

Albert grabbed Scout and headed into West Sunbury and covered the one mile quickly. The general store was busy and surrounded by wagons and buggies with their teams tied to the hitching posts. Albert tied Scout to a ring on the side of the store and ran in and to the back to find Mr. Breadon. Locating him, Albert told him he was Albert Eshenbaugh and then poured out the story of the shootings, the dead bandit, and the nature of the wounds to Mother and Will. He added that they needed a doctor, the sheriff, and the undertaker to come to the farm.

Mr. Breadon called out to two of his sons who were working in the store to come to his office. He dispatched one to run to Young's Funeral Home to bring Mr. Young over at once. The town no longer had a doctor, as the two once there had gone off to the war and only the dentist was in town. He was summoned as well.

Mr. Breadon had the telegraph station in the back of the store, so next he sent a message to the sheriff in Butler. He detailed that the highway bandit had ambushed the Eshenbaugh family, wounding two of them, and the gunman had been killed in the return fire. He asked the sheriff to ride out to the farm immediately.

The sheriff wired back that it was close to noon, and he had a good horse and would ride the nine miles as quickly as possible, so he wanted everyone at the farm by three p.m.

The dentist, Dr. McCarrier, was a member of a prominent family in West Sunbury. Though not a medical doctor, he did have good medical knowledge, and he immediately rode out to the farm.

When Doc arrived at about eleven a.m., Will insisted he examine Mother's wounds first. "Doc," as he was known, did not share his thoughts, but he was concerned about the swelling and the color of the exit wound on Mother. She seemed faint and was very pale as well. Her forehead was hot to the touch, and Doc was sure she was in shock. He worried to himself that this wound could cause a fever and probably an infection. He pulled a bottle of alcohol from his medicine bag and rinsed both the entry and exit wounds. He changed her bandages and wiped her forehead with cool water from the spring. After patting her hand, Doc said he would ride back tomorrow to check on her.

The sheriff rode hard and arrived before three p.m., and Will greeted him and offered him cold water. The sheriff then sat down on the front porch with Will and asked him to slowly recount the events of the shooting as well as to repeat the story of what Will had shared about the time in Butler when he was selling the potatoes. Carefully, the sheriff wrote notes and listened as Will recounted every detail of the violent episode.

Will then repeated the history of how he and Buckskin had met, giving details of how Buckskin and his filthy companion had shadowed Will and Mother from store to store in Butler back in November. Will related how the pair of criminals had followed him north out of Butler and attempted a robbery. Will decided it was time to come forward and share the part of the story he had not told the sheriff before. Buckskin and his accomplice were hiding behind the stack of railroad ties and quickly rode up to Will and Mother. Will told how the man dressed in black had pulled his gun on them, how Will had startled the black horse, throwing the man off his aim, and how Will had managed to shoot him and drop him off his horse.

Will reported that Buckskin then fired a shot from behind him, wheeled his horse around, and started up the hill. Will had used his rifle and believed he had hit Buckskin and maybe his horse as well.

Will did not go into details about dragging the dead thief off the road, stripping him, and floating him down Muddy Creek, as he figured the sheriff would ask more questions.

For a long time, they sat in silence. Finally, the sheriff said, "Son, how old are you? You sure have seen a lot for a young man."

Will replied that he would soon be seventeen. The sheriff said he was surprised, assuming that Will must be into his twenties. He asked Will what happened after that shooting, and Will gave him a very short version of how he decided to leave and join the Union Army, how he had gone to Kittanning first and then floated down the Allegheny River to Pittsburgh. He explained how he was shipped off to Harrisburg and then to the Shenandoah Valley and that he had ridden with General Philip Sheridan, who commanded all the Union cavalry in the campaign against the Confederates throughout 1864 all the way through to their surrender at Appomattox Court House in April.

As Will finished his report, the undertaker rode up on his wagon, pulling a hearse. The sheriff said he needed to see the body as he wanted to get back to Butler before nightfall. Will led them up the hillside to where the body of the buckskin shooter lay on the ground. The sheriff and the undertaker examined the corpse, and the sheriff commented that it was a very good shot, that it had hit the assailant right in the middle of the forehead. The sheriff told the undertaker to load up the body and bury it in the pauper's grave in West Sunbury.

The sheriff turned to Will and said, "I see no reason to file charges against you for either this shooting or the one from last winter with his partner. It certainly appears that both men were hardened criminals out robbing innocent people. Frankly, it makes Butler County a better place to have these two scoundrels in the grave."

Will walked back to the farmhouse, happy to know the sheriff would not press any charges against him. He collapsed in a rocking chair on the front porch, his shoulder throbbing in pain.

38

Will She Pull Through?

Over the following week, Doc rode out every morning to check on Mother. Realizing she was in significant pain, the doctor brought her doses of laudanum, an opiate-based painkiller. Doc did not realize—based on limited knowledge of the time—how addictive opium could be. Will was alarmed to see how lethargic Mother had become.

After five days, Will pulled Doc aside to ask him what was in the medicine and was causing her to be so lethargic. He asked if she was slipping away from them. Doc said he wasn't sure because he had never prescribed this much laudanum over this long a period.

The next time Doc examined her wounds, Will looked over his shoulder. Having seen numerous injured men in his time in the army, he was pleased to see her wounds appeared to be healing, and the color around the wound on both the entry and exit points now had a healthy pink shine. Will asked Doc to stop giving her the laudanum for a few days and see how she felt. Her fever seemed to have broken, and her temperature felt normal when Will wiped her face with a cool rag.

It took almost another week without doses of laudanum for Mother to begin to act normal. She was extremely weak after the prolonged time in bed and the effects of the laudanum. Gunshot wound treatment was limited to using alcohol to clean the wound and lint to pack it. Fortunately for Mother, no organs had been hit, and Doc had used generous amounts of alcohol on her wounds, as well as Will's, a process that had advanced considerably during the Civil War.

———※———

As the month of June rolled on, Will's shoulder wound healed nicely. He started regaining mobility and found he could do more chores around the farm, although some resulted in more pain than he had expected. He was also able to help Mother up from her bed and walk her to the outhouse. Her wounds were also continuing to heal, and slowly she regained her strength and balance. Once a week, two of the women from the church would drive out and help her attend to her bathing and personal hygiene. The ladies also took charge of the family's dirty clothes and washed them in a huge iron kettle over an open fire, then dried the wash on a clothesline. The highlight of their weekly visit was a full meal they brought with them that included freshly baked bread, a roast of beef or pork, and an apple or cherry pie.

One the first day of July, a letter arrived from Andrew.

My dear Mary Ann,

I first must tell you how much I miss you and the children and our home and farm. We have been on patrols here in Kansas territory almost daily since we arrived in late May. Some of our days are spent escorting wagon trains headed west, and other times we scout for hostile Indians, but so far, we have not encountered any.

I must tell you, too, that this is very boring land. There are few trees, and the land is flat as far as you can see. The days are hot, some say maybe over a hundred degrees and not much humidity once we are away from the river. I miss our hill and the views for miles from there.

The army is changing our ranks as we only have about 800 men here for the 1,200 troops normally. Our numbers are down due to losses to injury and disease as well as the desertions at the stop in Pittsburgh. My company is being absorbed into other companies, and I was just assigned to Company F. There are rumors that we may get to come home before the end of our enlistment in November, but we have not had any official word of that.

My health is good, and I wish I were there working the fields. I may have to seek work away from the farm once I am home to make ends meet. I hope not all jobs are filled by other veterans returning home long before the army lets me get back.

Please give my love to the children and tell them I look forward to Christmas at home this year.

Your loving husband,
Andrew

Mother gathered the family around over the supper meal and read the letter out loud to them. Everyone was thrilled to hear that Father was well and would be home by fall. The girls shrieked and danced around the kitchen, shouting with joy. Mother felt a tear roll down her cheek, and Will gave her a hug while Albert smiled ear to ear at them both.

After the dishes were cleared and stacked in the sink, Mother clapped her hands, and her voice rang through the kitchen like a hymn. "We're going to town for the Fourth! It's Independence Day, and we are going to celebrate it properly."

Will looked up from his cleaning. "You mean, a real outing? In town?"

"Yes," she said with a firm nod. "We're hitching the buggy, packing a picnic, and joining the others at the church lawn in West Sunbury. This family needs a day to remember that we're still whole and blessed."

Albert grinned. "Well, I'll be. A proper holiday—hopefully with food, games, and no chores."

The girls squealed with delight and darted around the kitchen, already chattering about watermelon and pie.

By mid-morning, the buggy creaked its way up the gentle hill that crowned West Sunbury's churchyard. The town green was alive with color—red, white, and blue bunting fluttered from porch rails, while families strolled beneath fluttering flags. The scent of roasting pork and sweet corn drifted on the summer breeze.

"There," Mother said as she pointed, shading her eyes beneath her wide-brimmed bonnet. "That patch of shade under the sycamore. Perfect."

Will nodded and reined in the buggy. He jumped down, unhitched the horse, and tied it where the grass was tall and lush. The horse nickered in approval.

Albert hauled the picnic baskets down, while the girls climbed down from the buggy, already chasing a hoop down the dusty street, their giggles trailing behind them.

"I haven't seen them this happy in . . . well, since before," Will murmured as he spread the blanket on the soft grass.

Mother settled down beside him, her eyes following the girls. "That's what today is for. A moment to feel peace again."

Reverend Decker's voice rang out across the lawn. "Children! To the church steps for sack races and the three-legged run!"

As laughter and cheers filled the air, Will leaned back on his elbows, letting the warmth of the sun soak into his bones. It was the first day in years that he didn't feel like a shadow from the war hung over them.

When the bell rang for the blessing, everyone gathered under the wide branches of the old elm. Reverend Decker raised his hands. "On this day," he called out, "we remember the freedom hard-won by sacrifice and give thanks for the grace to gather here together. Let us bow our heads." He said a prayer of thanksgiving, ending with all those gathered saying, "Amen!"

Later, bellies full and spirits high, Mother pulled out the grand finale—a glistening apple pie.

Albert whistled. "If freedom had a flavor, that'd be it."

Will nodded his agreement and took a big slice for himself.

In time, the sun began its slow descent, casting long golden shadows across the lawn. The women who had helped nurse Mother back to health gathered around her, embracing her and marveling at her strength.

"I never thought I'd see you out and about this soon," said Mrs. Withers, pressing her hand to Mother's. "We all prayed for your healing."

Doc leaned on his cane nearby and gave a nod. "She's as tough as anyone I've patched up, that's for sure. And you, too, Will—you're lucky that shoulder healed clean."

Will smiled faintly. "Luck or Providence—maybe both."

By dusk, the buggy was loaded, the horse hitched, and the girls—rosy-cheeked and drowsy—bundled under a light blanket. Will offered Mother his hand.

She took it with a grateful smile. "This was a good day."

As they rode home beneath a sky streaked with orange and lavender, not one of them spoke. The silence was peaceful, not heavy—an unspoken agreement to savor the rare joy of it.

July passed in a blur of sun and sweat. Thunderstorms rolled in every few days, soaking the crops and keeping the fields green and full. Will and Albert worked from dawn till dusk—cutting hay, stacking shocks of wheat in the fields, hauling it into the barn loft.

Each swing of the scythe, each lift of the bundle, brought the rhythm of life back to the farm. Hard work, honest work—the kind Will had missed during his many months of blood and battle.

One morning in early August, Mother stepped out onto the porch with a letter in hand. "It's from Andrew," she said, her voice trembling just slightly.

Will and Albert dropped their tools and hurried over. She read aloud:

Dear family,

It looks like we'll be heading home—maybe by the first of September. Our company's been relieved of patrol duty. There's talk that one unit will head up into the Dakota Territory, but I pray it won't be mine. I'm ready to be done with war and see the farm again. I can hardly wait to see you all.

With love,

Father

Will exhaled slowly. "He's coming home."

Mother folded the letter to her chest and closed her eyes. "Thank you, God."

The late August heat clung to the fields like a wet shirt. The wheat was in, the barn stacked to the rafters, and the air held the golden weight of summer's end.

On the afternoon of August 28, just as the sun dipped below the ridge, a figure appeared at the end of the lane. No one noticed at first. The girls were churning butter inside, and Will was splitting wood out back.

Mother wiped flour from her hands and stepped onto the porch to toss out the dishwater. She froze.

A Union soldier, dusty and tired, stood at the bottom of the steps. His blue coat was faded, his boots caked in road dust. He took off his kepi.

"Mary Ann," he said.

Her pail clattered to the porch boards. "Andrew?" Then she screamed, "Andrew!"

The screen door banged open behind her as Mother came running, followed by Will and Albert.

Andrew barely had time to drop his pack before he was surrounded—arms flung around his neck, hands grasping his arms, laughter and tears and disbelief all pouring out at once.

"You're really here!" Will shouted, gripping his father's arm like he might vanish.

"I promised you I'd come back," Andrew said, smiling through the tears. "I just didn't say how long it'd take."

Mother reached up and cupped his face with trembling hands. "Welcome home, my love."

Andrew pulled them all close. "I'm home. Right where I belong."

Author's Note

Honoring My Heritage

The title of this novel, *Up the Shenandoah*, is a play on words. Most rivers in North America flow southward, so "up the river" generally meant going north. However, the Shenandoah River in Virginia flows north through the Shenandoah Valley, so "up the Shenandoah" meant going south.

That was the goal of the Union Army in 1864 when General Grant took over the Union forces and sent General Sheridan and his cavalry south from northern Virginia to try to take the Confederate capital in Richmond.

My great-grandfather Andrew Harvey Eshenbaugh enlisted in the volunteer 14th Pennsylvania Cavalry that was being formed in Pittsburgh under Colonel Schoonmaker, who had risen from private to colonel and had connections to Governor Curtain to raise twelve hundred volunteers.

Andrew was thirty-seven years old when they formed in November 1862 and signed up for a three-year enlistment. The history of this outfit was documented in a book commissioned by Colonel Schoonmaker. He had quite a story to tell, starting as a young enlistee private who rose quickly in rank and met with the governor of Pennsylvania, who gave him authority to go to Pittsburgh and recruit his cavalry. For his bravery in leading the attack in the fortified position at Third Winchester in September 1864, the colonel received the Congressional Medal of Honor, as did Captain James Duncan, who was killed in the same battle.

Andrew Eshenbaugh returned to the farm in Clay Township, near West Sunbury in Butler County, following his discharge in August 1865. He farmed for several years, but by 1870 he had apparently gone to St. Louis, Missouri, seeking work. This was evidenced by an ad run in newspapers, including one in Boston, where his wife, Mary Ann Dixon Eshenbaugh, ran a notice looking for him. It read that she was "seeking information on Andrew Eshenbaugh, last known to be headed home from St. Louis, but not known if by rail, boat, or walking."

One can only imagine her worry and angst as she awaited his return. He is not shown on the 1870 census but is listed in the records again in 1880 as being on the farm.

Mary Ann must have been a tough and revered woman. Dixon, her maiden name, was given to her son William Dixon Eshenbaugh (my grandfather) as well as a son of Albert Eshenbaugh, who was also named William Dixon Eshenbaugh, a grandson named William Dixon McCarrier, and on down to my generation as my late brother was named Charles Dixon Eshenbaugh.

Will was my paternal grandfather, William Dixon Eshenbaugh. Not a lot of facts are in evidence of William's time in the 4th PA Cavalry. There is a William Eshenbaugh on their roster, but there are not many details on his service.

Based on stories told by my father, J. Arthur Eshenbaugh, and my cousin Dale Waldenmyer, Will did make his way to the western Pennsylvania oil fields shortly after the end of the Civil War and became a master driller. He spent his career drilling in Venango, Butler, Armstrong, and Allegheny Counties. Other family members, including the other William Dixon Eshenbaugh, Albert Eshenbaugh, and another William Eshenbaugh followed the oil fields north into western New York and then south into West Virginia and then later to Oklahoma, Texas, and finally by the 1920s to the massive oil fields near Los Angeles. Both Albert and the cousin, William Dixon, died there in the 1920s and are buried in Los Angeles.

My research uncovered another fascinating family connection. Robert Gillespie Campbell was a thirty-seven-year-old man, the father of seven children, and a farmer in Cherry Township, just north of West Sunbury and only three miles from the Eshenbaugh farm. Robert had been praying for guidance, torn between eking out a living for his family and his conscience telling him to do the right thing: support President Lincoln in his call for seventy-five thousand more troops from Pennsylvania. Making the decision easier was a Union Army offer of a $300 sign-up bonus plus $12 a month pay. This was far more than his small farm made to support his growing family. Finally, on February 29, 1864, Robert mustered in and was sent to join the Fifty-Ninth PA Infantry. After a short training period, the infantrymen were deployed to the front. By the end of March, Robert was sent by railcar into Virginia, and in the first week of April, he saw his first day of combat in the Wilderness.

Unfortunately, Robert and over a dozen other green rookie soldiers were surrounded by Confederates, taken prisoner, and marched south to a new and hastily constructed prison at Andersonville, Georgia. Robert would die there in August 1864, starved to death and subjected to disease and barbarous conditions so atrocious that when the war ended, the commanding officer of Andersonville was convicted of war crimes and hung by the Union. Three generations later, a great-granddaughter of Robert Campbell would marry the oldest son of Will. She was my mother, Ethel Irene Campbell Eshenbaugh.

Will also had uncles serving in North Carolina under General Grant. His father's brother John was a veteran in the Fifty-Ninth Infantry. He was wounded in his leg, captured, and shipped to Andersonville, where the leg was amputated. He survived and returned to West Sunbury after being released at the end of the war in 1865 and became a successful lawyer.

Another uncle, Thomas, also a veteran infantryman serving in the Union Infantry in North Carolina, was captured and shipped to Andersonville. While he survived, Will never saw Uncle Thomas again.

As for the homestead of Andrew and Mary Ann, there remained only a few stones marking the location. They were located on part of the farm where I grew up, one mile south of West Sunbury. Just north, there still stand the barn William Dixon built in 1889 and a house that came from Sears and Roebuck and was erected in 1890 for his marriage to my grandmother Sara Ada McNabb. I grew up there, and my father was born in that house and lived in it his entire ninety-eight years. He died in 1990, and as part of the estate, a portion including the house and barn were sold off. The family retained sixty acres and then sold about half of that to Kevin Eshenbaugh in 1992, with the balance sold to my sister Janet Eshenbaugh Campbell and her husband, Jerry. In 2024, they sold to their granddaughter Sara Hull Young, who built a house near to where Andrew and Mary Ann had their barn. Note, too, that she spells her name the same way as her great-grandmother Sara McNabb Eshenbaugh.

As for me, I thought I might be a history teacher when I was sixteen, but after exposure to the world of home building and land development, I switched my focus to an education in finance, real estate, and business management, beginning my college education at Penn State in 1960. My cousin Wally Waldenmyer became my mentor when I was sixteen, and along the way he shared a lot of the verbal history, especially about my grandfather William Dixon Eshenbaugh. Wally encouraged me to capture as much family history as possible. Through his encouragement and my father's longevity (born in 1892 and lived until 1990), I was also able to add much of the family's unwritten stories.

I also accessed Ancestry.com and put together a 702-page family tree and narrative. In turn, that inspired me to organize and lead a "graveyard crawl" in 2024. Over forty family members traveled from as far away as Florida, South Carolina, and Ohio to spend a Saturday morning touring two cemeteries in West Sunbury, Pennsylvania, where we paid homage at twenty graves of family members.

I felt much more connected to my ancestors from this study of the family tree and made a trip to the town of Eschenbach in Bavaria, Germany. There, we traced the story of Andreas Eschenbach, who was born in that town in 1710 and came to America in 1740. He is our first ancestor to land in Pennsylvania.

I fear that many families do not know their roots. With the mobility of our society—from the early pioneers who braved the frontier to the mass migration and expansion following World War II—countless connections to lineage have been lost. But knowing where we come from matters. It grounds us. Family history gives us a sense of identity, a thread of continuity in an often-disconnected world.

Understanding the hardships our ancestors endured, the values they held, and the legacies they left behind deepens our appreciation for the life we now live. It reminds us that we are part of something larger than ourselves—a story still unfolding. In an age when the past can feel disposable, preserving these stories and passing them on to future generations may be one of the most meaningful acts of stewardship we can offer.

Acknowledgments

Much gratitude goes to my parents, J. Arthur Eshenbaugh and Ethel Campbell Eshenbaugh, both teachers in one-room schools, who spent countless hours sharing their stories and memories with me as a child growing up on the farm in the era before television.

Along the way, my cousin Dale "Wally" Waldenmyer, who was nineteen years my senior, provided a tremendous amount of family history. He was the bridge to the connections with William Dixon Eshenbaugh, our grandfather, as Wally spent several summers on the farm working as a youth alongside my father and our grandfather.

Thanks go to my coach, David Brown of Southwestern Consulting, who gave the push needed to bring this project forward. I am always appreciative of my wife, Lynda Keever, the former publisher of *Florida Trend* magazine. She provided hours of support and guidance, as she does with all of my endeavors. Special thanks also to our daughter, Kristina Chutz, who helped with the research.

I also appreciate the guidance of my Colorado-based editor, Keith Wall. Thanks to modern-day technology, we worked mostly by email and texting to steadily move through ideas, drafts, and changes to bring my ideas to this book.

About the Author

William "Bill" Eshenbaugh was born in Butler County, Pennsylvania, and grew up on the farm where his great-grandfather Andrew and great-great grandfather John Eshenbaugh homesteaded in the early 1800s and where Andrew built his house and lived his adult life and where Andrew's son William Dixon Eshenbaugh built his house in 1890 in preparation for his marriage. In this same house, Bill's father, Arthur, was born in 1892 and lived until he died in 1990. The family still owns portions of the farm and several of the current generations have built houses on parts of the farmland.

Both of Bill's parents taught in one-room schools, and he thought early on in life that he wanted to be a history teacher because of his love for history, especially about the Civil War. Life took a different direction. Bill graduated from the Pennsylvania State University in 1964 and spent a career in real estate.

He makes his home in Florida on a horse farm near Tampa, where he has enjoyed being married to Lynda Keever for thirty-seven years. She's a retired publisher of *Florida Trend* magazine and Bill deeply appreciates her for her assistance with getting this book completed.

Bill has traveled the Shenandoah Valley from Winchester south to Richmond, where both his great-grandfather and grandfather Eshenbaugh rode with the Pennsylvania Calvary during the Civil War. Bill was able to visit a number of the battlefields, including the Third Winchester where great-grandfather William fought, as well as Spotsylvania Courthouse where his great-grandfather William McNabb was mortally wounded, and in the Wilderness area, where his great-great-grandfather Robert Gillespie Campbell, a newly recruited Pennsylvania infantryman, was captured and shipped to the infamous Andersonville prison where he died in August 1864.

Bill developed his love for the land, working on the farm as a youngster and a teenager. He has had a very rewarding career in Florida as a land broker, assisting ranchers and farmers in selling their land.

His hobbies include saltwater fishing, and long-distance (hundred-mile-plus) horseback trail rides.